CAMP SYLVANIA

MOON MADNESS

ALSO BY JULIE MURPHY

MIDDLE GRADE NOVELS

Dear Sweet Pea
Camp Sylvania

TEEN NOVELS

Side Effects May Vary
Dumplin'
Puddin'
Pumpkin
Ramona Blue
Faith: Taking Flight
Faith: Greater Heights

CAMP SYLVANIA

MOON MADNESS

JULIE MURPHY &
CRYSTAL MALDONADO

BALZER + BRAY

An Imprint of HarperCollinsPublishers

Balzer + Bray is an imprint of HarperCollins Publishers.

Camp Sylvania: Moon Madness
Copyright © 2024 by Bittersweet Books LLC
Illustrations by Emma Cormarie (pages 45, 62, 133, 153,
161, 183, 214, 228, 235) and Jenna Stempel-Lobell
All rights reserved. Printed in the United States of America.
No part of this book may be used or reproduced in any manner
whatsoever without written permission except in the case of
brief quotations embodied in critical articles and reviews. For
information address HarperCollins Children's Books, a division of
HarperCollins Publishers, 195 Broadway, New York, NY 10007.
www.harpercollinschildrens.com

Library of Congress Control Number: 2023943350
ISBN 978-0-06-334726-7

Typography by Jenna Stempel-Lobell
24 25 26 27 28 LBC 5 4 3 2 1
First Edition

To John, Mary, and all the stories to come
—J.M.

To friends who love us through every (moon)
phase of life —C.M.

You!
(Yes, you!)

ARE CORDIALLY INVITED
TO RETURN TO THE ALL-NEW

If you're receiving this voucher, you are one of the LUCKY FEW
affected by last summer's UNFORTUNATE INCIDENT. 😃😃😃

The brand-new owner of CAMP SYLVANIA
would like to formally apologize and invite YOU
to make FUN NEW MEMORIES.
(And forget last year's MASS FOOD POISONING!)

This voucher* entitles you and ONE FRIEND
to a FREE SESSION at the ALL-NEW
CAMP SYLVANIA!

Experience a holistic approach
to fun and well-being! Charge your crystals!
Enjoy a healing sound bath!
Sample our PROPRIETARY MOON WATER!
It will *transform* you!

CHAPTER ONE
Maggie

I had to read the invitation three times before I believed it was real.

Last summer, when I waved goodbye to Birdie, the best camp counselor of all time, who helped us all defeat her vampire sister (long story), I for sure thought we'd see each other again one day, but not at Camp Sylvania. I had no plans to set foot in that place again.

Until I did.

I didn't even plan on going back to a summer camp at all this year, but you know what they say about cats and curiosity and all that. So here I am, just miles away from the start of my second summer at Camp Sylvania, except this time my bestie is coming along for the ride and this is actually going to be the best summer of our lives!

"This packing list is so bizarre," Nora's mom, Miss Cammie, says as she mulls over the orientation email on her phone for the millionth time since we crossed the

Texas state line yesterday morning.

Nora's stepdad, who she and her brothers refer to as Stepdad Steve, grips the steering wheel of the brand-spanking-new minivan he bought last week for his recently doubled family as we wind down the familiar road to Camp Sylvania.

Miss Cammie continues. "I packed your obsidian . . . it's in the snack-size ziplock baggies next to your allergy medication and face sunscreen . . . but I couldn't find tourmaline anywhere."

Nora throws her head back against the headrest and pretends she can't hear her mom even though her Bluetooth headphones totally died an hour ago.

I accidentally make the most awkward eye contact ever with Stepdad Steve in the rearview mirror and then look away.

"Um, it's no biggie, Miss Cammie," I say because I can't stand silence for too long. "My mom bought mine from some crystal shop on Etsy, so I have plenty to share. Besides, I'm pretty sure there's no crystal store on County Road 29." And then I snort. Ugh. That was unfortunate. (The snorting, I mean.)

I sink low in the bench seat in the back of the van where Nora and I have camped out for ultimate privacy. "Those headphones died back at the roadside fudge depot, and you know it," I whisper to Nora.

She slumps down beside me and pulls her glossy pink headphones down around her neck. "I'm at max parent capacity right now," she tells me. "And I hate this minivan. It's so corny."

I cringe. "I saw that Stepdad Steve even put one of those stick figure bumper stickers on the back with the whole family."

She rolls her eyes and lets out a helpless whimper.

I never used to think my parents were embarrassing, but now just getting dropped off at school every day sends me into a brain spiral as I try to troubleshoot any potential humiliation that might play out. It doesn't help that Dad's car makes this rattling sound that basically draws the entire school's attention to us.

But a minivan? That's a whole other level of mortification. And not just because it's a minivan! I can never open the door the right way and crawling out the back is basically a tripping hazard waiting to happen. When Stepdad Steve dropped us off in it on the last day of school, Nora had to beg him to let us get out at the end of the drop-off line. Trust me when I say you don't want to embarrass yourself on the last day of school. It's all anyone talks about for the whole summer and on the first day back, you're the butt of every joke until the next poor kid embarrasses themselves.

"Hey, you were talking in your sleep last night," Nora says. "Something about electromagnetics?"

"My EMF reader! A.k.a. electromagnetic field reader. The ghost-hunting device I got with my birthday money. I had a nightmare that I left it at home." I swipe a hand across my forehead. That really would have ruined the whole summer, to be honest.

"Well, you seemed pretty stressed out in your dream, which makes sense, because everything about ghosts is nightmare inducing."

"This again?" I ask. "Come on. After last summer, how can you not open up your mind to the paranormal? It's, like, all I can think about."

She shivers. "More like after last summer, how can you even stand to think about it?"

I reach for her hand and the matching plastic friendship bracelets I made last weekend sit side by side, reunited in a picture-perfect moment. Last night, I gave Nora hers when we got into bed at the hotel. The plan was to wait until we were alone in our cabin, but I couldn't wait any longer. "You know this summer is going to be totally different, right? No more Sylvia. And the new camp director sounds really cool. A little hippie-dippie, but they brought back the blob *and* the Jet Skis!"

"I've never ridden a Jet Ski before, and I gotta admit, that sounds pretty cool. Mami still hasn't signed my waiver though."

"She'll give in. I've only done it once, and it was basically the best five minutes of my life. Plus, we're going to be sharing a cabin for two whole weeks. You'll basically forget your new loser stepbrother, Darren, even exists."

"Did I tell you Mom and Stepdad Steve are letting him take over the game room as his bedroom this summer before he leaves for college just because the guest room is only big enough for a twin bed and he's supposedly 'a growing young man'? What about the TV and the PlayStation and the Nintendo Switch and the old air hockey table? The couch in the family TV room is so fancy that my mom won't even let me drink clear Gatorade on it. How am I expected to lounge under those circumstances?"

"RIP game room," I say solemnly. "We had some truly epic *Mario Kart* tournaments in those hallowed halls."

Nora takes a calming breath in through her nose and out through her mouth. "But you're right. This summer is going to be the best. We might not be going to Camp Rising Star, but we have a whole two weeks without parental supervision. And no kidnapping vampires this year, so that's already a win. It's going to be the most normal, chill summer ever. Like, so normal, it'll be a little boring."

"I'm pretty sure boring isn't something we should aspire to, NorBear."

"Okay, well, maybe we'll have a crush or two." She gasps. "Or maybe people will have crushes on *us*."

My lip curls. No thanks. "Ooooooor maybe we'll see a ghost and I'll get the chance to test my new ghost-hunting equipment."

She rolls her head to the side and gives me her best *really* look.

"You know it's all real," I whisper. "Vampires, ghosts . . . river monsters!"

"River monsters? We have zero proof those are even a real thing."

"Okay, but they probably are. This summer is all about fact-finding for me and it starts with getting proof that ghosts are real. And then maybe river monsters too."

Howie Wowie was the elusive and sometimes helpful ghost from Camp Sylvania last summer, and my experiences with him and the world of vampires has had me searching high and low for evidence of the paranormal for the past year. Howie was a former camper and ultimate daredevil who met his untimely demise after a Jet Ski stunt gone wrong. Now he's known to wander the grounds in his tie-dye T-shirt and neon swim trunks.

"Normal," she reminds me. "Chill."

"Totally," I say.

"I hope the outfits I packed are cute without trying too hard. You know what I mean?"

I shrug, wishing I knew how to care about all the things that Nora is interested in this year. Crushes, clothes, TikTok dances. "Hey, did you pack the cherry blossom string lights you got for Christmas for our cabin?"

"You know it," she says. "And those kitten face masks and that picture of us from second grade in the macaroni frame."

"Sweet. I packed the *Wicked* poster and . . . okay, this was supposed to be a secret, but I got us boba Squishmallows with my allowance. Matcha for me and strawberry for you!"

Nora shrieks with excitement before sinking even farther down into her seat.

I peer up to see Stepdad Steve smiling at us as the trees

on either side of the road grow thicker.

"No one knows me like you do," she says with a sigh.

"Ditto, bestie," I tell her with certainty. This is going to be the summer Nora and I have dreamed of for a really long time, and nothing's going to get in our way.

"We're here!" I sing as we pass under a huge banner that reads *LUNA LUPOWSKI WELCOMES YOU TO THE NEW AND IMPROVED CAMP SYLVANIA!*

We both turn to look out our respective windows and a soft gasp catches in my throat as I notice a familiar ghostly presence sitting on a tree stump and waving.

Howie! Yes! This summer is already the best.

Over the last year, I'd begun to wonder how much of last summer was a dream, or at least a tall tale. None of it seemed real after we got home. Had there really been a camp ghost? Did Sylvia actually farm a whole camp of kids so she could build her own immortal beverage empire? Surely the International Society of Slayers had been a figment of my imagination. But then I have to remind myself that it was real. It was all real.

And this summer I'm going to prove it. Starting with Howie. I even brought my mini Polaroid camera to try to capture a picture of him. Film doesn't lie! (And I don't technically have a cell phone yet.)

The minivan rolls to a stop in a clearing that's become a temporary parking lot for incoming campers. My whole body is buzzing and the moment the car is in park, I fling myself out the van door. "Do you smell that?" I ask Nora. The muggy air mixes with a soft breeze drifting in from the lake.

"The geese poop?" she asks.

"No! Freedom!" I close my eyes and inhale deeply through my nose. "Okay, and maybe a little bit of geese poop."

"Did someone say geese poop?"

I open my eyes to see Logan trotting toward me with a tall lanky guy with a dark brown complexion and hip wire-rimmed glasses a few feet behind him. "Logan! I thought you weren't getting in until tonight!"

He grins, loping over to me with a side hug. "Surprise! Turns out my cousin failed language arts and couldn't walk at graduation, so my grandma got me"—he turns back to the boy behind him—"or, well, us on the earlier flight."

Logan's voice sounds . . . different and he's at least six inches taller than he was last summer. He reaches around my shoulders and his armpit smells like a forest made of spearmint, which is a vast improvement over most of the boys at school. My stomach gurgles, but I'm pretty sure that's just because I'm hungry.

"Did you bring the EMF reader?" he asks quietly.

I immediately geek out. "I can't wait for you to see it," I tell him. "It is the single coolest thing I have ever owned."

"This summer is going to rule," he says definitively. "This is my neighbor and oldest friend, Jesse. Since my brother couldn't come this summer, my grandma offered him our extra voucher."

Jesse shrugs with a grin. "My parents can't say no to free stuff. Plus my dad won a cruise for two at work and this was a better option than staying with my great-aunt. She loses her dentures. A lot."

Behind me, Nora clears her throat.

"Oh, hey, Logan, you remember Nora, right? My bestie forever."

Jesse steps forward and holds a hand out for Nora to shake. "Good to meet you, Nora."

Her cheeks redden as she tries to suppress a smile.

Logan nods. "Hey, Nora! Last time I saw you, you were dive-bombing a vampire on the set of *The Music Man*! So epic."

Nora's smile falters. "Some things are better left forgotten, if you know what I mean."

Logan looks from me to Nora and then back to me. "Yeah, I'm pretty sure last summer is going to be seared into my brain for eternity."

And he's right. Last summer was totally horrific, but unlike Nora, I don't want to move on by forgetting it all ever happened. Because even though it was terrifying, I have never felt so alive. Talk about a rush of adrenaline! Besides, sometimes the only way to get over your fears is to embrace them.

Now if I could just get Nora to do the same. . . .

CHAPTER TWO
Nora

Best friends don't get jealous. Best friends don't get jealous. Best friends don't get jealous.

I repeat this over and over in my head as I watch Maggie and Logan gush—like, full-on animated arms and big eyes and loud laughing—about how they can't wait to dig into all things supernatural this summer. Since when are they so close? And why are they so focused on the paranormal?

Okay, fine. Maybe I am a little jealous. I try to swallow it down as best I can. It's just that this summer is supposed to be about *Maggie and me*, not *Maggie and Logan*, or *Maggie and Logan and Jesse* and definitely not about ghosts or river monsters or bloodsucking V-words. The thought of them still sends a chill down my spine!

Don't get me wrong: I'm *all* for summer camp adventures. But less like the scary monster kind, and more like the cooler eighth-grade kind. I want adorable summer outfits and s'mores and crushes Maggie and I can ogle. I'll even allow a spooky campfire story. But after last summer's "unfortunate incident," I've been really looking forward to a summer camp do-over.

Thankfully, from the brief glimpse I got on the drive in, the new Camp Sylvania seems to have been scrubbed of everything from last year. Mami even said she was impressed by the makeover, and she's skeptical of pretty much *everything*. Not that I blame her. My older brothers, Junior and Sebastian, are forever testing her. One time, they stuffed a bunch of fake spiders into the cabinet with all her spices so they fell on her while she was cooking. She hasn't trusted a closed cabinet since.

In this updated version of camp, all of Sylvia's branding is gone, replaced with all things Earthy-crunchy: the giant banner welcoming us to camp looked like its letters had been embroidered on burlap, there are pastel-colored garlands of lavender strung from some of the trees, New Age music is playing softly through the PA speakers, and I swear someone is burning sage. There's no way anyone is getting kidnapped at a place that has a healing sound bath.

Logan must catch me taking in our surroundings because he motions around us and asks, "What do you think of the new look? Kind of . . . a lot, right?"

"Yeah," Jesse says, looking less than impressed. "I'm just waiting for the new camp director to pop out from behind a tree and force us to hold hands and become one with nature or something."

I laugh quietly. Okay, Jesse is sort of cute.

Maggie wrinkles her nose. "Totally. What even is that smell?"

"That's sage," I say. "And I don't know, I think the new look is okay?"

When there's a beat of silence, I self-consciously tug at the end of my braid.

"The flowers are really nice," Maggie offers. Then she glances over at Logan. "Buuuut it *is* a lot different."

I can tell she's trying to make us both happy.

"It will be great for you girls to have a chance to actually spend the summer together," Mami says. "I hate the idea of my baby being alone in the woods, so knowing she already has good friends like you to keep her company makes me feel better."

There's so much wrong with what Mami just said I don't even know where to start: Logan is really more Maggie's friend than mine, I don't really know Jesse, and—ugh—I'm not a baby who needs to be looked after. She's always acting like I'm still six years old.

Instead of saying anything, I bite my tongue, knowing arguing with Mami is no use. She's never met a fight she didn't win, and being given The Look—a stare from Mami that's so sharp it could slice through rock—in front of everyone sounds mortifying.

"My great-aunt has also been nervous about this whole camp thing," Jesse offers politely. "She's kind of a conspiracy theorist though. She told my parents this camp used to be run by vampires who—"

"Ha!" Logan lets out a sharp laugh and claps Jesse on the shoulder. Maggie's eyes go big. "That great-aunt of yours. Always falling down some kind of Facebook rabbit hole!"

"Your aunt sounds like she has quite the imagination," Mami muses, raising an eyebrow.

My eyes dart around the grounds hoping I might see something that could inspire a different conversation—one that's not about me being a baby or about the supernatural—when I notice a girl across the parking lot, leaning up against a tree. She's reading what appears to be manga, and I am instantly drawn to how effortlessly cool she looks.

From her Doc Martens, which I can spot from a mile away, to her leather jacket (which is maybe not the most practical choice outdoors in the middle of summer, but oh my gosh!!!), to her dark hair streaked with strands of blue, this girl *radiates* chill. She's even rocking a deep purple lipstick that looks like something an influencer might wear. I need it!

"Promise me you'll be safe," Mami continues, tucking one of the curls that's escaped from my French braid behind my ear.

I tear my gaze away from Cool Girl and huff. "Obviously."

Mami sighs. "A little less attitude would be great."

I plaster on a bright, fake smile. "Better?" I ask through gritted teeth.

She smiles back and pinches my cheek. "There's mi

princesa. Oh! And I was able to get you an appointment with Dr. Hernandez when we get back so we can get you a new set of braces like we talked about."

"*Mami*," I groan, glancing quickly between Maggie, Logan, Jesse, and Cool Girl in the distance. "Can we not?" I really don't need the whole world knowing that I was getting braces for a second time. Getting my braces off before school last year was the best day of my life, but by spring break my teeth were almost as crooked as they were to start with. Dr. Hernandez blamed it on not keeping my braces on long enough, but I had to admit I wasn't very good at wearing my retainer either.

"What?" Mami asks innocently, as if she really has no clue what she's just said. "I think you'll look adorable with braces." She touches my upper lip. "And maybe we can get this little mustache waxed too."

It's then that Stepdad Steve finishes unloading our luggage and rejoins us in the lot. As far as stepdads go, Steve is . . . fine, I guess. He listens to NPR podcasts and classical music, he wears polos and khakis even on the weekends, and he loves bird-watching and giving people an enthusiastic thumbs-up. Harmless, really. It's less about him and more about how his presence in our lives changed literally *everything*. I felt like I had just started getting used to the Whaley household being me, Sebbie, Junior, and Mami, and only seeing my dad on the occasional weekend, when boom! In came Stepdad Steve and his (annoying) son Darren. As if I needed another dad or brother. Even though Stepdad Steve tries really hard, sometimes it's almost too much, and I find myself internally cringing when he enters a room.

Right now, though, I'm actually grateful for his presence. At least we can stop focusing on my crooked teeth.

"All right, I think that's everything," he says, dusting his hands off. "Thank God the camp staff is delivering your bags to your bunks. Took me two whole trips to drop off Nora's luggage at the main office!" Stepdad Steve winks at me, letting me know he's only teasing, but his comment feels like an extra jab in an already irritating morning.

"Well, I did have to pack for practically a month," I say defensively. Camp is technically only two weeks, but I needed to pack for every possible scenario.

Mami playfully swats at Stepdad Steve's arm. "Hey, don't judge—a girl needs options!"

"How else is Nora going to have the best wardrobe at camp?" Maggie asks. Then she turns to Logan and Jesse and adds, "She really does. Wait till you see."

And that makes me soften a little. Thank goodness for my bestie.

I bump my shoulder with hers. "Thanks, Magpie."

Stepdad Steve puts his hands up in surrender. "I was only joking! I *fully* support your packing habits." I glance over at Maggie and give her my subtlest eye roll. She stifles a giggle. "Now, should we get going and let these kids settle into their summer?"

Without another word, Mami throws her arms around me dramatically and smothers me in kisses, and I wish the ground would open up and swallow me whole, because hello? I'm almost an eighth grader! I don't need my mother hanging all over me like I'm a little kid. Maggie's so lucky that her parents said goodbye to her back in Texas.

I hug Mami back half-heartedly before wriggling out from under her death grip. "It's only two weeks," I remind her. "I'll be back soon."

She wipes at her eyes and sniffles. "Okay, mija. I'll miss you." Mami wraps Maggie in a big hug, too, then pulls me to her and squeezes us both. "And take good care of each other."

I catch Maggie stealing a glance at Logan as her cheeks go pink.

"Okaaaay." My voice comes out whinier than I intend, but can she just please *go* already?

"I love you," Mami says, blowing me another kiss.

"Love you too, Ma," I reply impatiently, practically shooing them into the car.

Stepdad Steve offers a corny thumbs-up before he and Mami get into their minivan. A moment later, their car pulls away, leaving a cloud of dirt in its wake.

I breathe a sigh of relief as I watch their car grow smaller in the distance.

This is it. Summer!

I grin over at Maggie, Logan, and Jesse. "Should we go get our cabin assignments?"

Maggie loops her arm with mine. "Let's go!"

My body hums with excitement as we make our way into camp to check out where we'll be bunking. I just know I'll be with Maggie—we're the same age *and* I was the friend she chose to bring along for her free week. How could they not put us together?!

We practically run down the path to the main camp building, arm in arm.

And there, on the bulletin board, is our destiny. My chest squeezes as I walk up to the bunk assignment sheet.

I scan for Maggie's name, which is always before mine:

Name: Maggie Hagen
Cabin Assignment: Waning Crescent

"Oh no . . . ," Maggie murmurs next to me.

"What? What?" I try to read as quickly as possible. And then I see it:

Name: Nora Whaley
Cabin Assignment: New Moon

My heart sinks. "We're not in the same cabin." I can feel my whole body deflate. How can this be happening?

"Ugh! This stinks." Maggie frowns, then looks at me. "We even made a bunkmate request!"

"There goes our plans for decorating the perfect room," I

say, as if that's what I really care about, but my voice cracks slightly on the last word—total betrayal.

Maggie must be able to see right through me because she squeezes my arm reassuringly. "We'll hardly be in our cabins at all. And we'll be spending all our free time together for sure!"

I brighten a little at that. "That's true. What cabin did you guys get?"

Jesse points toward his name on the sheet. "Waning Gibbous." His voice is surprisingly deep, and when I look over at him, I notice he has one eye that's brown and one that's green.

Logan finds his own name and smiles. "Me too!" Then he scrunches his face. "Aw, man. You're not going to prank me, are you?"

"Are you saying you don't want me to stick your hand in a bucket of warm water to make you wet the bed . . . again?" Jesse asks.

"That never happened!" Logan quickly assures us. The tips of his ears go bright red. "And no, I absolutely don't want you doing that. Ever!"

Jesse laughs. "Oh, fine. Guess I'll have to torture our mystery roommate with my pranks instead."

"That's a relief." Logan turns to me and Maggie. "Sorry you guys aren't bunking together."

"We don't need to be in a cabin together to have the best

summer ever," Maggie says with a firm nod. "Right, Nor-Bear?"

She seems a lot more sure about this than I am, but I nod anyway. "Right."

An airy voice comes over the PA. "Welcome, campers! Please head to your bunk to meet your cabinmates, then grab some dinner before joining us all on the camp lawn at seven o'clock sharp for our welcome meeting. See you soon!"

I look over at Maggie. "Guess this means we should split up."

"Yeah. I guess so."

Logan points behind Jesse. "I think your cabin is the same way as ours, Maggie." He points in the opposite direction. "And, according to that sign, yours is that way, Nora."

Ugh. Of course.

"Want us to walk with you to your bunk?" Jesse offers.

"Oh, um. I think I'll be all right," I say. "Thanks though."

"Time to meet our roomies, then." Maggie gives me a small, nervous smile. "See you on the lawn in a little bit?"

I smile back. "Definitely. Just promise you won't like your bunkmates better than me." I'm only half joking.

Maggie rolls her eyes. "Like that could ever happen."

Then, with a hug and a wave, she and I head in opposite directions.

As I walk toward my cabin, I take a closer look at the handmade bracelet from Maggie. Now that we're not bunking together, I really appreciate having a reminder that Maggie will always be there for me. I don't even mind that the bracelet colors clash a little with my pastel tank top and shorts! Talk about true friendship!

A flash of movement up ahead interrupts my thoughts. I stop dead in my tracks, peering in the direction of whatever I just saw. But nothing is there.

I swear I saw something! It even kind of looked like a tall, creepy figure lurking through the woods. I shudder at the thought.

Why do I suddenly feel like I'm not alone? The hairs on the back of my arm stand up and my heart starts to pound. What if that *was* a vampire? Or one of those river monsters Maggie mentioned?

Come on, Nora, I remind myself. *Monsters are so last summer.*

I steady my breathing the same way I've coached Maggie when she has major stage fright. In, two, three, four. Out, two, three, four.

Then, before I enter my cabin to meet my bunkmates, I smooth my ruffly tank top and fix the headband in my hair. I want to make a good impression, not one that hints at the fact that I believe in scary monsters (even if it's true).

So I put on my warmest smile and open the door, ready to greet the campers I hope will soon become my friends.

Only, I'm surprised when the cabin is . . . empty?

Mostly, anyway. My pile of watermelon-print luggage is

beside the first bed, closest to the door, and then I see her.

Cool Girl.

In my bunk.

"Hi!" I say, and my voice comes out like a squeak. I instantly worry I sound like a total baby, so I clear my throat and try again with a casual, "Hey."

Cool Girl looks up from her bed, where she's sprawled out reading the same manga she had been enthralled with earlier. She gives me a nod.

"Oh, hey. Are you the roommate?" Her voice is low and raspy, kind of like she has a cold but somehow not a gross one. How is it that even her voice is awesome?

I shrug, motioning at the other empty beds. "One of, I guess. I'm Nora."

"Well, Nora, you lucked out. I'm Claire, your one and *only* cabinmate. We get this gigantic bunk to ourselves."

My eyes go big. How is that even possible? The website said the camp would be at capacity for this summer session, so I was expecting a full cabin of three—and even dreading it a little. My brothers are always in my space as it is, so I wasn't thrilled at the idea of having to share absolutely everything with strangers.

"But how?" I ask, and Claire smirks.

"It's pretty much the only good thing about being the camp director's daughter. My mom is desperately trying to get me to go over to the dark side and embrace her lifestyle of crystals and sage—so this is one of her ways of trying to win me over. Or maybe she's just nervous I'll be a bad influence on other campers," she explains. With a sigh, she adds, "She spends a good chunk of her life trying to make mine worse, I swear." Then she arches an eyebrow at me. "Ready to help me spend the summer trying to guilt my mom into more special privileges?"

I grin. Maybe this summer won't be so bad after all.

CHAPTER THREE
Maggie

Logan and Jesse veer off up the path to their cabin while I head down the familiar winding walk to my cabin, Waning Crescent, closer to the lake.

I pull up short at my cabin and immediately recognize the fading three on the front door that has been partially covered up with a pastel pink moon. Cabin Three! Just like last year.

"Home sweet home," I mumble to myself as I push the screen door open.

"Surprise!" two voices I'd know anywhere scream as Kit and Evelyn jump out from behind their beds.

Some sort of vulturelike screech comes out of my mouth. "Holy bats! I thought y'all were going to an equestrian camp in Massachusetts!"

Kit frowns. "Well, it turns out I'm allergic to horses. And all the other camps I wanted to go to were full."

"And I already had my heart set on summer camp with

Kit," Evelyn adds in her crisp British accent. "So we decided to surprise you with a Camp Sylvania reunion."

"Minus the vampires," Kit says with a snort.

"I can't believe you're both here." My lower lip begins to tremble. The three of us stayed in touch over the school year, but Kit and Evelyn got super close and even saw each other when Evelyn visited her dad in Kansas City over spring break while Kit's family was visiting her sister in college. I don't feel left out or anything, especially since I have Nora. Besides, after what happened last summer, I am eternally bonded to them both.

"Well," I say, "if I can't bunk with Nora, at least I've got you two."

Evelyn grimaces. "That might sort of be my fault. I wrote a very strongly worded email explaining why the three of us needed to share a cabin."

"But Nora can totes hang out with us anytime!" Kit chimes in.

"Totally. Nora is one of us for sure."

Kit starts to put her sneakers on. "I've got bad news though. Word on the trail is that a family of mice nested in the motors of the Jet Skis, so no Jet Skis for us two years in a row."

I let my backpack drop from my shoulder with a thunk. "Seriously?"

"The good news though," Evelyn says as she slips on her sandals, "is that there's a chicken coop this year and the first campers to visit the coop get to name the chickens. And both of my parents are anti-four-legged family members, so this might be my only shot at naming an animal before I turn eighteen and adopt nine cats."

"I was thinking a vampy name as an homage to last summer." Kit taps her chin thoughtfully. "Maybe Renesme . . . We can wait for you to get settled if you want?"

"No, no," I tell her. "You two have chickens to name." I hold my arms out for a hug and they both rush me until we're a tangle of arms and giggles. Maybe I can talk to Captain B about squeezing a fourth bed in here for Nora. Then this would be truly perfect.

After they run off to the chicken coop, I haul my suitcase on top of my bed and begin to unpack. Mom packed outfits for me in ziplock bags since her most recent obsession is hyper-organization and space saving because of some Netflix series she binged. Thankfully I got a new suitcase this year, so at least last year's floral print hand-me-down with broken wheels was replaced by a galaxy-printed hardshell case.

Nora was totally mortified that I let my mom pack my outfits, but the way I looked at it was that it was one less thing to do. And it's just clothes. They'll just get sweaty and dirty.

"Knock, knock," a voice calls from outside and then in a Dracula accent, "You must invite me in before I can cross the threshold of your humble abode."

I lean back to see Logan standing outside and quickly shut my suitcase to hide my underwear, sports bras, and the clear baggie full of pads that my mom helpfully labeled FEMININE HYGIENE PRODUCTS.

"Come in!" I call back to him as I plop down onto the edge of my bed.

"Did you hear there's a chicken coop this year?" he asks.

"Oh, yeah. At least they're not in danger of becoming vampire smoothies this summer," I say a little glumly.

He sits down on Evelyn's bed across from me. "Girl cabins smell way better than boy cabins, just FYI."

"Do you have a large sample size of girl cabins to prove that hypothesis?" I ask.

"Uh, seeing as we're not technically allowed in each other's cabins, not exactly. But I can confirm that while Jesse might be my neighbor, he still smells like BO masked with body spray after running to catch our flight today." He sniffs at his armpits "Okay, maybe that's me."

I laugh all giggly and high-pitched. My stomach suddenly feels floaty and warm at the thought of Logan being in my cabin. It's so weird.

"Hey, Maggie?" he whispers even though it's just us. "Is it strange that I was sort of disappointed when we showed up and there were no vampires or blood bank?"

I lean toward him and in a low voice say, "Uh, no. Like, I know they're dangerous and all that. But . . . it was exciting too, ya know? It's like I've been walking around with this huge mind-blowing secret and no one else has a clue. They don't even know that the supernatural is right there under

26

their totally mortal noses!" Wow. I just said way too many words way too fast.

Logan is quiet long enough for my stomach to drop, but then his eyes light up and he grins. "Honestly, if I didn't have you to email for the last year, I would have thought I made the whole thing up."

"Right?" I ask excitedly. "Nora wants to pretend the whole thing didn't happen."

"My brother too."

I nod. "I can't blame them. Evelyn and Kit have just magically moved on like it was no big deal and here I am poking my head in every dark corner, hoping something jumps out to scare me."

"I can't believe I'm about to admit this," Logan tells me, "but sometimes I sneak out in the middle of the night and walk to the cemetery at the end of my street. For no reason!"

Oh my gosh. Walking through a cemetery, hunting for ghosts in the middle of the night sounds like a dream come true. And doing that with Logan . . . well, the thought makes my cheeks tingle. "Have you seen anything otherworldly?"

He sighs. "One night I thought I did, but it was just the maintenance man making his rounds."

"You know, Brock Shepherd on *America's Most Haunted* always says that—"

"'The supernatural appears to those who are open to it,'" he finishes. "Brock is a genius. Probably the coolest adult of all time!"

"Of course you love that show! You have killer taste." Has he somehow gotten even cooler since last year?

He nods. "Maybe since we're both open to the supernatural, that will double our chances of witnessing something this summer."

"Yes! This!"

He stands up from Evelyn's bed. "Okay, okay, I better go track down Jesse. He's never been farther than a ten-minute walk from a Target or McDonald's. He's probably already lost in the woods, searching for a GameStop."

I wave as he opens the door. "Haunt you later!"

Logan's brow furrows for a moment before he shrugs and walks out onto the path.

I throw myself back against my mattress. *Haunt you later? Really?*

After I unpack, I go in search of Nora but get caught up with Evelyn and Kit, who start telling me about chickens and their ideas for names. Then it's dinnertime and Nora is already sitting at a full table.

I wave at her and she waves at me, but she looks like she's having so much fun talking to new people that I suddenly feel weird going over there and interrupting just to say hi.

After dinner, as I walk down to the lawn, the moon hangs low in the sky while the sun slips past the horizon. Nora sits at the bonfire with a girl in black from head to toe. I race over as fast as I can to rescue her from who I'm guessing is the new weirdo bunkmate she's stuck with.

"Is that Maggie Bananas?" a voice calls.

I spin on my heel to find the one and only Captain B, a.k.a. Birdie, tending the fire just a few feet from Nora. "I was nervous when you weren't on my airport pickup list," she says as I dash over.

Captain B drops her fire poking stick and catches me in a hug. I have to admit, it gives me the warm fuzzies to see her again. Mom said Captain B would be back this year, but I couldn't believe it until I could see her for myself.

"Nora's family decided to road-trip it this year, so I came with her," I tell her. "But Mom says to tell you hi!"

She laughs. "As if she and I don't already text every other day." Mom and Captain B go way back—they were bunkmates at this very camp ages ago.

"So, uhhh . . . any word from Sylvia?" I ask in a low voice.

Captain B shakes her head. "She sent our parents a postcard from Boca Raton over the holidays."

For as much as I sort of kind of hoped for some more vampire action this summer, it is comforting to know that Sylvia—the former camp director/influencer turned vampire is far, far away from us. Social media wasn't very kind to her either, after her big plans to turn this place into a kid blood farm imploded—even though that wasn't the story that the rest of the world knew.

Sylvia's mysterious disappearance was a major news story for a few weeks after camp ended. Some people thought it was a publicity stunt. Others thought she went to rehab. Some even worried that she'd encountered some foul play. Only a small handful of us knew the truth: that Sylvia was on the run from the vampire slayer council and promised to never show her face at the camp again. The one good thing about vampires? They can't break a promise.

I catch a glimpse of Nora laughing and wave to her. She turns to the girl beside her and says something before trotting over to me.

"Nora!" Captain B exclaims. "I'm so happy to have you back this year as a full-fledged camper! And I see you met Luna's daughter and your bunkmate, Claire."

Did she just say Luna's *daughter*?

Nora nods. "Claire is very cool. Apparently, last year for a school project she coded her own app where you take a quiz to find out your own personal style aesthetic and then it gives you shopping recommendations. That's basically like having a personal stylist!"

Wow. Claire is so cool. Insert eye roll. I wasn't jealous, okay? (Well, maybe a little.)

"That kid is an overachiever," Captain B confirms. "Well, I better get back to this fire so we can get going with s'mores."

I follow Nora over to where Claire sits, the light from the flames dancing across her face like she's in some kind of angsty music video.

"Claire, this is my friend Maggie," Nora says.

"*Best* friend," I clarify.

"Cool," she says as we sit down.

Logan makes his way through the crowd with Jesse trailing behind and I wave him over to the empty spot on the log beside me.

"Have they started handing out marshmallows?" he asks.

"And as soon as they do, I can prove to you that a marshmallow is best served on fire so that the inside is turned to molten hot sticky goo," Jesse says.

Logan throws his hands up. "For the millionth time, the purpose of toasting marshmallows is to *toast* them."

"Don't get too excited," Claire says from the other side of Nora. "Luna's idea of s'mores includes toasted pineapples covered in cinnamon."

Jesse smacks Logan's shoulder. "You said this place wasn't a fat camp anymore, but they don't even have real s'mores."

"Luna isn't about diets or anything," Claire explains. "She's just really into all things au naturel and finding your inner beauty yada, yada, yada."

"How do you know so much about this Luna lady?" Logan asks.

"She's her mom," Nora says, and a weird part of me feels like she should have shared this info with me ASAP so I didn't have to get the scoop from Birdie. But it's not like there was a chance to do so before now, I guess.

"Any special perks with being the camp director's daughter?" I ask in an effort to prove that I am totally cool with sharing my bestie.

Claire rolls her eyes. "Nothing that I would count as an actual perk."

"But we *do* have a cabin to ourselves!" Nora gushes, and the two exchange a pleased look.

Nora and Claire start to geek out over some fashion TikToker from Japan who they both love, and Jesse and Logan are arguing over who's better at *Skyrim*.

I sit there quietly, swiveling my head from side to side as I catch little snippets of each conversation, but never fully getting in on either.

From the other side of the bonfire, Kit and Evelyn wave after settling onto the last open log, just big enough for the two of them. Everyone is paired off. Why do even numbers suddenly matter so much? Last year, Kit, Evelyn, and I were an inseparable tripod, but they've gotten closer, which is totally cool, and I was supposed to have Nora. . . .

Once the fire has reached its full roaring potential, a new camp counselor with a wiry beard and bushy eyebrows passes out skewers with—sure enough—chunks of pineapples dusted with cinnamon sugar.

Despite the grumbles, we all give it a go and approach the fire to roast our pineapples.

Beside me, Logan shakes his head. "I like pineapples as much as the next kid, but something about this feels a little familiar, if you know what I mean."

He's referring to last summer and Sylvia's Scarlet Diet, which forced us to subsist on red foods only. Definitely the first of many red flags. (Pun intended!)

We hold our skewers out over the fire while other kids line up for organic graham crackers (that look suspiciously like corkboard) and chunks of chocolate bark that look solid enough to break a tooth.

"I think I'll stick to the pineapple," I say.

Beside me, Nora takes a bite of her caramelized pineapple. "Whoa! That is delish!"

I blow on mine before chomping into it. Crunchy on the outside and juicy on the inside. "Okay, that's pretty good," I say through a mouthful.

Logan makes a show of holding his nose as he tries his, and I can't help but laugh.

"You know," I tell him, "when you do that, you look like the host from that new show, *Haunted History*. What's his name? Bowen something . . ."

"Bowen Powers!" Logan waves his hands excitedly. "Did you see the episode where they summoned the ghost of Benjamin Franklin?"

"Yes! Nora," I say, "this is the show I've been trying to get you to watch."

She shrugs. "If I watched every show you recommended to me, I wouldn't even have time to sleep."

Logan snorts. "Who needs sleep when there are ghost-hunting shows to watch?"

"All those shows are rigged anyway," Claire says. "Right, Nora?"

I know it's totally unfair, but I think it's safe to say I am one-hundred-percent certain that I do not like this girl Claire.

"Those shows *are* pretty awful," Nora admits.

Well, that gets my nerves all prickly. I step in front of her so she can't slip away too easily. "But you *know* all that stuff is real."

Nora stares at me for a moment, and I can see Claire watching us from the corner of my eye.

Finally, Nora shrugs. "Who knows for sure?" She steps around me and follows Claire to the outermost logs.

"That was weird," I say, but when I turn to Logan, he and Jesse are laughing at some inside joke about living in a pineapple under the sea. Evelyn and Kit are giggling about their very messy s'mores and I'm just . . . alone.

Okay, I tell myself, this pity party is over. This was silly. I wasn't about to let some new goth girl scare me off hanging out with my best friend.

I start to make my way over to Nora and Claire when a whistle sounds, and a voice rings out, "Welcome, campers!"

CHAPTER FOUR
Nora

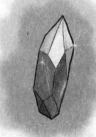

At dinner, Claire introduces me to a whole group of people: twin girls with matching black hair and brown eyes named Rosie and Posie Wood and their bunkmate Sara Park, a tall boy who goes by Big Liam, and a (cute!) light-skinned brown boy with the most perfect smile named Elijah. I don't know how she's managed to befriend this many people already, but I'm not complaining.

Yet Claire shudders the moment she hears her mom, Luna, say, "Welcome, campers!"

"Here we go . . . ," Claire whispers to me.

As far as looks go, Claire and her mom seem like total opposites. While Claire, with her blue-streaked hair and dark eyes, is comfortable in all black clothes, a leather jacket, and black eyeliner, Luna has long, light blond hair with a few strands braided around her head like a crown; a flowy white bohemian dress; and not an ounce of makeup, at least that I can see. The only thing they seem to have in common is matching ivory skin and freckles.

After her welcome, Luna casts her gaze around the circle of campers, as if wanting to personally say hello to each and every one of us. Then she offers a warm smile.

"I am thrilled to have you here at the new and improved Camp Sylvania. Now, I know last summer was incredibly challenging for many of you." Luna's voice is soft and gentle like a lullaby. "However, I want to reassure you that we understand how that must have impacted you, and we applaud your generous hearts and spirits for giving this camp another chance."

I have to admit that it's nice to hear someone acknowledge how hard last summer was. Between Maggie's new obsession with the supernatural and the way pretty much everyone else has acted totally unbothered, I was beginning to feel embarrassed that I wasn't over it yet.

"I can assure you that we have rid this camp of all of the negative energy from the previous owner, whose name I will not dignify by speaking aloud, and I want you to know, above all else: you are safe here."

Her words ring in my ears like a melody. I am safe here. Meaning I don't have to worry about being kidnapped by vampires, and everything will be fine.

She continues. "This summer, we will prioritize the *good* by exploring the joys of living naturally and existing in our most authentic state."

Claire bumps her shoulder into mine. When I look over

at her, she rolls her eyes and mouths, *So dramatic*. I have to hold back a laugh. Captain B eyes us and points toward Luna, reminding us to pay attention.

"Here at Camp Sylvania, we reject all animal products and chemicals. All campers will follow a strictly curated— healthy but *delicious*!—raw, all-natural diet. We will refrain from using any artificial fabrics or products."

There are a few whispers, but Luna presses on.

"That includes chemical face washes, sunscreens, deodorants, bug sprays, and acne creams."

The whispers grow louder, and I have to admit, I'm suddenly feeling a little skeptical too. Why would anyone think it's a good idea to get rid of sunscreen, deodorant, and bug spray at an outdoor camp in the middle of summer?

And, sorry, but no acne cream? That feels almost mean!

I look over at Maggie, who appears just as outwardly mortified as I feel inside.

"Is she serious?" I whisper.

Maggie shakes her head. "I can't believe how strict they're being!"

Claire leans in. "Told you my mom isn't as great as she seems."

Luna claps her hands together to regain everyone's attention.

"I hear your concerns, and I validate them. This may seem shocking for those of you who are not used to living a clean, synthetic-free life, but worry not. In place of these chemical-laden products, we'll be using items made from this area's most incredible natural resource: moon water!"

She reaches for a chain that had been hidden inside the neckline of her dress. Then she untucks the pendant and holds it up for us all to see. It's a small glass vial filled with an iridescent liquid that almost looks like it . . . glows?

The comfort I'd been feeling a few moments earlier disappears, and I nervously start to fiddle with the bracelet Maggie gave me, twirling it around my wrist again and again. Why does this place always have to have something to do with magic?

"You see, I knew Camp Sylvania was the perfect location for my all-natural camp because of the large deposits of quartz crystal in the lake bed. The crystal energizes the lake water, which—when charged by the powerful light of the moon—takes on incredible healing and purifying properties." Luna hugs the vial of water to her chest. "I hope you know how lucky we are for this opportunity!"

While I'm struggling to process all this new information, I notice that Maggie and Logan are standing, trying to get a better look at the glowing liquid clutched in Luna's hand. I wish I could just relax and be as fascinated as they are.

"To ensure we all have access to this magnificent resource, we have set up a moon-water charging station. Counselors?" At Luna's direction, a few of the staff members rise and move toward a large, mysterious, tarp-covered object on the lawn.

All at once, the counselors lift the tarp to reveal a

humongous tub made of quartz crystal that's filled with the same glowing liquid from Luna's vial. The surface of the shimmering water has been sprinkled with flower petals and lavender, making it look like something from one of those day spa websites Mami is always looking at.

"This bath will charge our moon water each night," Luna says. "And I encourage you all to take your own free vials of moon water to apply to your skin before bed, or to add in small drops to your drinking water. There are also pamphlets available that explain more and, of course, I am happy to talk to you as well! Don't be shy. Use this moon water liberally and often, and you'll be amazed at how quickly you see results from its purifying properties. Now, let's have a positive summer embracing all of the gifts from this generous universe!"

As Luna finishes her welcome speech, there's a half-hearted round of applause from the campers, who seem a mix of confused and awestruck. Counselors start to pass out vials of moon water. Captain B stands and hands us each our own.

I take mine, carefully turning the cool glass container over in my hand and inspecting the iridescent liquid up close.

"So, what'd you all think?" Captain B asks.

"Luna seems sweet?" I offer.

"So do berries, but plenty of those are poisonous in the wild," Claire jokes.

Captain B shoots her a look. "Claire," she warns.

Claire shrugs. "I'm just saying!"

"It was okay I guess, but I don't get the no-acne-cream thing," Logan says. Then he quickly adds, "Not that I need it or anything. But I'm sure some kids do." His cheeks flush pink.

"Yeah," Maggie agrees. "The new rules are sort of weird, but I'm super curious about this moon water stuff."

"Change is always difficult to adjust to, but I'll tell you, Luna's been a great leader and boss so far. She seems to really care for you kids." Captain B points over at Claire's mom, who is laughing with some of the younger campers. I have to admit, I don't think I'd ever seen Sylvia mingle with campers beyond trying to harvest them all for our blood. Luna may be a bit much, but at least it seems like she means well.

Captain B continues. "Now, you all head back to your bunks before it gets too late. It's lights-out soon. And let me know how you like your moon water! I tried it myself, and it seemed to clear up a patch of stubborn eczema I've had all summer." She lifts her left elbow to show us a clear patch of skin—no eczema in sight. "Anyway. Night, all. Be good."

We say our goodbyes to Captain B as campers flood out of the bonfire area. I start to walk with Maggie, Claire, Logan, and Jesse.

"Can you believe it? Moon water! With healing powers!" Maggie is practically beaming. "Sounds pretty paranormal to me."

"I *knew* Camp Sylvania 2.0 was hiding something good."

Logan grins and offers Maggie a high five, which she happily accepts.

Jesse raises his eyebrows and looks over at me. "What do you think about all this, Nora?" Then he quickly adds, "And Claire?"

"I don't know. . . ." I say, genuinely unsure. My head still feels like it's spinning from all this new information.

"I hate to break it to you guys, but I'm pretty sure moon water is just regular water that my mom makes look pretty," Claire explains. "She means well, but it's mostly her wishful thinking that she's 'one with the universe' or whatever."

Logan holds up his vial. "Well, if that's true, then why is this *glowing*?"

"Vitamin B," Claire says.

"Pretty sure that doesn't make water glow," Jesse argues.

Then Claire points to one of the lights illuminating the crystal tub. "It does with black lights. It's, like, little kid science experiment stuff. Look it up if you don't believe me."

At that, Maggie's face falls. "But it fixed Captain B's eczema. . . ."

Claire nods. "That's also one of the benefits of Vitamin B."

"So Luna's just lying?" Jesse asks. "About the healing properties coming from the moon?"

"I mean, *she* doesn't think she's lying. My mom really does believe in all that stuff, and I can tell you for a fact that she loves living an all-natural life. Her natural diet stuff actually isn't all terrible, considering. Weren't the toasted

41

pineapples sort of good?"

"They were, but we're pretty anti-diet in my house," I admit. "Mami has always been really against the idea of restricting foods. She'd flip if she knew this was going on."

Maggie sighs dreamily. "Lucky. My mom will be all for it when she finds out."

"So . . . the moon water potentially being paranormal isn't a thing, then?" I ask.

Claire shakes her head. "It's total nonsense."

Maggie suddenly stops walking. "It's not." We all stop, too, and listen as she lowers her voice. "What happened last summer was *real*. And very much paranormal."

"Hey, I heard the rumors about last summer, and I'm not sure what to believe, but—" Claire says, putting up her hands as if to show she means no harm. "All I'm saying is that what's happening *this* summer is my mom's attempt at trying to make us all sing kumbaya around the campfire and not use makeup so we can embrace our inner beauty or whatever. Nothing more. And definitely nothing paranormal."

A silence falls as the two of them stare at one another for a moment. Logan and Jesse exchange an awkward glance. I figure I should be the one to try to break the tension.

"Both things can be true," I offer.

Maggie turns toward me. From the look on her face, I can tell she's upset that I haven't automatically rushed to her defense.

How can I, though, when I really want what Claire is

saying to be right? Isn't it better if the moon water is nothing more than tricks of the light and vitamins?

Claire slings her arm around my shoulders. "Exactly! Nora gets it."

"Fine," Maggie mutters, crossing her arms. "I should head back to my cabin."

"We'll walk with you," Logan offers. "C'mon, Jesse."

We exchange awkward goodbyes and I fall in step with Claire as we head back to our bunk. I feel really bad that I seem to have hurt Maggie's feelings, but what about *my* feelings?

As I reach for the door handle to let Claire and me into the bunk, I notice my wrist looks strikingly empty.

Then I realize: Maggie's bracelet! It's gone!

"Oh no! Be right back!" Before Claire can even ask where I'm going, I race back to the bonfire. A knot forms in my stomach as I go. No, no, no, no, no! I can't upset Maggie *and* lose my treasured friendship bracelet all in one night.

When I make it to the bonfire, it's so much darker than when we left just a few minutes before. The area is deserted except for some smoke billowing from where the fire had been put out. Even the lights around the moon-water tub have been turned off for the night.

Without a flashlight or a phone, I use the moonlight to look for my bracelet. First I check the log where I had been sitting, but when I come up empty-handed, I drop to all fours and feel through the grass.

Please let my bracelet be here somewhere.

After a few panicked moments of finding nothing, my fingers finally land on something smooth, cool, and, as Luna would say, synthetic. I snatch it up and bring it right up to my face, the knot in my stomach untwisting when I recognize the pink, purple, and green braided strands. My bracelet!

I clutch it to my chest and whisper, "Thank goodness."

Just as I turn to head back to my bunk, there's a splashing sound from behind me. When I whip around toward the noise, all I see is a dark figure scampering away from the moon-water pool.

I freeze.

Could that be a vampire? The tall, creepy figure I thought I saw earlier? Something even worse?

"No," I say out loud. I take in a deep breath and repeat the words that resonated with me most during Luna's welcome. "I am safe here."

Claire even assured us there's nothing weird going on here, and I believe her. I *have* to.

But I still run the whole way back to my cabin.

CHAPTER FIVE
Maggie

I wake up to the sound of wind chimes and a gentle voice. "Good morning, campers. This is Luna speaking. It's time to welcome a new day full of possibilities."

"Is that the voice of God?" Kit groans. "Are we dead?"

Evelyn removes the silk eye mask that matches her bonnet as she sits up on her elbows before reaching over and pinching Kit's arm.

"Ouch!" Kit shrieks.

"Still alive," Evelyn and I say in unison.

I yawn as my body slithers out of bed and in search of clothes that almost match. "Do you think we can expect these wake-up calls every morning?"

Luna's voice chirps in from the speaker system outside. "Remember these next two weeks are about reconnecting with your most natural self. Please don't forget to bring your crystals inside after charging them in the moonlight. For a list of appropriate crystals to charge in the sunlight, please visit the camp bulletin board. Lastly, the word of the day is *cleanse*. Breathing workshop begins after breakfast and then you'll take part in breakout sessions."

"I don't understand why we need help breathing," I grumble as I tie my shoes and then pull my unbrushed hair into a ponytail. Not brushing your hair and not having your mom run behind you to check if the bristles on your toothbrush are wet is probably my favorite part about camp. It's like a vacation for your hygiene.

Okay, I guess that's kind of gross, but whatever. Gross I shall be. Or all natural as Luna would call it.

A knock pounds at the door and that really wakes up Kit and Evelyn for real this time.

"Good morning," Birdie's voice calls.

"Uh . . . hello," I say as I open the door to find not just Birdie but also Luna waiting there. "Is everything okay?"

"All is well," Luna says sweetly as she steps past me and into our cabin, followed by Birdie. She wears a long lavender maxi dress and no shoes—like at all. How do her feet not hurt on the gravel? "We're here to collect any . . . unnatural or synthetic items you might have brought to camp with you. Contraband."

"Everyone is getting bunk checks," Birdie tells us as she rocks back and forth on her heels. "I'll do some looking around, but if you'd like to make this easier and just turn in whatever you think might violate the rules, that would be very cool of you."

"We're looking for food, toiletries, and anything else you might have with unnatural dyes or chemicals," Luna explains. She holds up a basket of items. "We've stocked the bathrooms with fully organic soap, shampoo, and conditioner, but we're also delivering moon-water sunscreen made with goats milk and coconut oil and moon-water bug spray made with essential oils."

"Those sound . . . homemade," I say.

"With the utmost care and intention," Luna confirms.

"Right," I say. "Just—just give us a minute."

"Of course," Birdie says as she starts on Kit's side of the room.

The three of us turn our backs to them both, making silently frantic faces. I was totally not prepared for this.

"Okay, girls," I say way too loudly. "Let's get all of this stuff together that we totally don't need because we're embracing our natural selves this summer, right?"

I kneel down next to my bed and Evelyn and Kit do the same so that we can sort of communicate from under our bed frames.

Evelyn pulls out her toiletry bag and throws her hands up frantically. She digs out a small jar.

"What do we have here?" Birdie asks as she pulls out a bag of homemade Funfetti cookies from the trunk at the end of Kit's bed. "These do look delicious."

"They contain artificial dye," Luna remarks as she takes the cookies and puts them in a trash bag.

Kit whimpers. "My sister made those for me."

"And you can have them back at the end of camp," Luna says. "Trust me, with all the preservatives in them, they'll be like new."

Sorry, I mouth to Kit as I dig around under my bed, hoping to find what I'm looking for before Birdie does. It feels weird to hide something from her, but she is super on board with Luna's program, so a girl's gotta do what a girl's gotta do.

I may be the kind of girl who goes to sleep with wet hair and whose eyes water at the thought of mascara and who is definitely guilty of skipping a shower after PE, but there is one thing in my toiletry bag I absolutely cannot live without.

I dig through my duffel bag until I find the old ziplock baggie full of two-in-one shampoo, face wash, toothpaste, loose bobby pins, and peppermint-scented body wash from my Christmas stocking.

There she is! The little white tube with my name on the side. My medicated acne cream, a.k.a. the little potion that saved my life and my chin this year.

Sure, everyone gets acne, especially at my age, but last fall when my breakouts started to actually *hurt*, my mom took me to the dermatologist, and I found out I had something called cystic acne. The doc gave me a prescription for this magical cream that I would sell every single one of my belongings for. Even my ghost-hunting equipment. (But definitely *not* my dog, just to be clear.)

The tube is a little too big to fit into my jean shorts pocket, so I look for another hiding spot.

There! In the corner of the screen window is a little hole big enough for me to push it through. I crawl over to the wall and pretend to use the windowsill to get up. I'm hoping I'm discreet enough so that no one notices me popping the tube through the tear in the screen.

"There you go, sweet, sweet, acne cream," I whisper. "I'll be back for you."

I stand up and wave my baggie in the air. "Here it is! I knew my toiletries were around here somewhere."

"Wonderful, Maggie," Luna says. "I really appreciate your forthcoming and willing energy."

She walks over to me as Birdie starts in on Evelyn's stuff. When no one but me is looking, Evelyn pops the little jar she'd taken out of her bag into her mouth. Her eyes widen as she shrugs at me helplessly.

Luna opens my baggie. "This deodorant has aluminum, which is just awful for you. And oh, this body wash is no better than rinsing in toxic chemicals. And this toothpaste . . . your poor, poor teeth must be about ready to fall out of your head."

"Oh . . . well, that sounds painful," I say.

Luna pats me on the shoulder. "Don't you worry. I've stocked the bathrooms with charcoal toothpaste, sugar body scrubs, and crystal deodorant."

"Oh, thank goodness," I say.

Birdie's brows furrow together as she shakes her head. "Looks like Evelyn is in the clear." Luna smiles, looking back and forth at each of us. "This was such a fulfilling experience, and I truly want to thank you three for your understanding and—" She stops mid-sentence and steps toward my bed. "Oh, look at this wonderful stack of books."

She eyes my summer reading on the paranormal, and I sigh with relief once I realize she hasn't noticed the acne cream outside my window.

I step back a little so she can get a better look. "Yeah, I'm really intrigued by all the things we can't see, I guess."

"How open-minded of you! I'm very impressed, Maggie." She picks up the first book, one called *Ghosted: The Story of How I Annoyed My Ghost into Leaving Me Alone*. Beneath that is my EMF reader. It detects electromagnetic fields, and lots of ghost hunters believe that ghosts can mess with electric activity.

Luna picks up the device by the antenna like it might melt her skin off. "Oh," she says. "Oh, dear. Maggie."

I turn to Birdie nervously, but she doesn't really seem to get that I'm kind of freaking out here. "Is there a problem?" I ask.

"Maggie, we certainly do have a problem," Luna says, like she's just found a dead body under my bed. "This is an electromagnetic field reader, and I'm sure you don't know this and that this is nothing more than a naive mistake on your part, but these devices can really interfere with your aura and the aura of those around you."

"Her aura?" Kit asks. "Is that something you can measure?"

Luna walks over to Birdie and drops my precious EMF reader in the bag. "Not all of us have that type of sight, but luckily I do. Come, come." She waves me over. "I'll check Maggie just to be sure. I can't be sure of your exact aura color without knowing more about you, but I can at least tell if your aura is crying for help. Everyone, close your eyes."

I do as she says, but squint so that I can still see what's happening.

She clutches the crystal around her neck along with the vial of moon water as she closes her eyes for a moment. Then with huge movements, she flings her arms out at me and makes whooshing noises. "Oh, oh, Maggie! You have a resilient aura." She nods. "This is good. This is very good."

"Cool," I say. "My mom calls me persistent. But that's mostly when I ask her if Nora can spend the night until she eventually snaps and says yes."

Luna eyes me like I'm an equation she would very much like to solve, and then she turns to Evelyn. "Dear, you haven't said a word. Is everything okay?"

Evelyn nods, and I can see the panic in her eyes. She's got some fancy jar of cream in her mouth and if she moves her lips, she'll be caught.

"Evelyn took a vow of silence," I blurt.

Evelyn looks at me, eyes wide in shock.

I grimace. Maybe not my best cover story.

Luna gasps and holds a hand to her chest. "A vow of silence! How attuned you must be. Have you decided how long it will last? Perhaps for the duration of camp? Or maybe you're aligning your vow with the lunar cycle?"

Evelyn points to her mouth and shrugs.

"Ah, yes, of course." Luna nods knowingly. "The silence. Silly me. Well, I look forward to hearing about your time in silence once you're moved to speak again."

Luna bows to us and walks outside, her bare feet crunching on the gravel (ouch!) as Birdie follows her.

Evelyn holds her hand out and the little jar she was holding in her mouth spills into her palm. "A vow of silence? Seriously? Thanks a lot, Maggie. Now I can't talk for at least the rest of the week."

"I'm sorry!" I tell her. "Maybe you can just say it was a morning meditation practice or something . . . I don't know. Half the words that come out of Luna's mouth are nonsense anyway."

Kit slumps down onto her bed. "Those cookies are definitely not going to still be good in two weeks. No matter what Luna says."

CHAPTER SIX
Nora

As it turns out, having a gigantic cabin pretty much to yourself is awesome. Claire and I wake up early to decorate *however we want*—no parents to stop us, no older brothers to prank us (me) by stealing our (my) things, nothing! What more could a girl want?

On my side of the room, I string up cherry blossom string lights, a Blackpink poster, and Playbills from the shows Maggie and I have been able to see at our local theater. I've also added a framed program from Sunnyvale Community Theatre Day Camp's production of *Annie*, which I starred in, because I have yet to experience a thrill like seeing my name written out in the lead role! I may not be at Camp Rising Star this year, but having these mementos on my wall remind me that I can handle anything as long as I put on a brave face. That's what I do every time I perform, right?

My desk is neatly organized with the crystals Mami packed for me, plus my huge collection of colorful pens, stationery and matching envelopes, stickers, and highlighters: perfect for writing letters home (even though I can't really picture my brothers Junior and Sebbie reading anything from me without making a stink face). My new strawberry boba Squishmallow from Maggie gets a place right on my bedside table next to my journal.

When I look over at Claire's side of the room, it's clear our styles are not all that similar. Her walls are plastered in posters of bands I've never even heard of, plus some really cool-looking manga art. While I have a collection of photos of me and my family and me and Maggie (including the one in the macaroni frame), I notice that Claire only has pictures of herself with her friends. There are no pictures of her with her mom or any family that I can see. Weird.

On her desk, she has a stack of books so high it seems like it's trying to reach for the ceiling. I decide it's safer to comment on that than the lack of Luna pics.

"Whoa, that's a lot of books! Are you planning to read them all this summer?" I ask, then cringe. Books are meant to be read, Nora—of course she's planning to read them all!

Claire looks over at the towering stack. "Yeah, I hope so. I need to find a way to keep myself busy since I can't do any coding without my laptop. I'm a fast reader, and it'll be nice to be able to escape all the woo-woo stuff of this place if it gets to be too much. And it will."

She comes closer to my side of the room, and I suddenly start to worry that everything I've put on display looks too babyish. Maybe all the colorful art supplies make me look like a kindergartener rather than a sophisticated bullet journal influencer.

"Is that washi tape?" Claire points at three cat-shaped washi tape dispensers lined up on my desk.

"Yeah! I'm kind of obsessed with writing supplies. You should see my collection at home." I laugh a little. "I had to narrow them down and choose only a couple to bring, but I think I did okay. That washi tape has little trees and flowers on it." I point at the one farthest to the left.

She reaches for the orange-and-white tabby cat dispenser. "Wait, is this one summer camp themed?"

"It is! It's got little tents, campfires, a canoe . . . silly, I know . . ."

"No way. These are awesome." Claire tilts her head. "I see washi tape at the store and stuff, but I never really understood what washi tape is for, you know?"

"I can show you." I grab my journal, flipping it open to a recent spread I'd made to mark the end of seventh grade. "Here. I use the washi tape as accents or to add photos and stuff onto the pages."

Claire reaches for my journal and a smile creeps over her face as she looks it over. "Your handwriting is so neat. It looks like a font!"

That makes me laugh. "Thanks. I fall deep down the bullet journal hole on TikTok sometimes." I leave out the part where I have to borrow my mom's phone to get on the app.

"I've been getting really into makeup tutorials lately," Claire says, handing me my journal. "I just found one about this amazing geometric eyeliner that I'm dying to recreate. I wish I had my phone to show you because I feel like you'd love it!"

"Defally!" I say to my absolute horror. "I mean, definitely. I was trying to say *definitely* and *totally* at the same time."

Way to go, Nora.

But Claire laughs it off. "Yeah. Defally."

Suddenly, someone is pounding on the cabin door. We both turn, and I scramble to let whoever it is in before they break in and ruin the door to our newly created sanctuary.

I'm surprised when it's Luna and Birdie.

And Luna is BAREFOOT.

"Good morning, girls!" Luna's voice chirps. "Bunk check. We're here to collect any"—she narrows her eyes at Claire—"*contraband*."

"Hope you're not hiding anything," Birdie says with a wink. They both step into our bunk.

Claire crosses her arms with a scowl. "Did you guys have to knock like that? You scared us for no reason!"

"Oh, I'm sorry, darling. Most of the campers were asleep when we arrived, so it's required a bit of a heavy hand," she explains. "We weren't expecting you two to be such early risers!"

I motion behind me. "That's my fault. I wanted to wake up early to decorate before breakfast."

Birdie looks around and lets out a low whistle. "Wow! *This* cabin deserves an award for best decorated." She gently nudges Luna with her elbow. "Don't you think, Luna?"

"It really is lovely," Luna agrees, and the compliment makes me feel warm. "Now, on to business: Is there anything you two would like to hand in?"

Ugh. I'd been dreading this moment since the announcement last night. I don't use tons of beauty products yet, but I have some basic makeup, and I am pretty attached to things like my deodorant and moisturizer. Plus, I had bought some pretty shimmer lotion I was super excited about using this summer! So long, dreams of looking like a glittery goddess.

"Just this from me." I grab my cloud-print toiletry bag and hand it to Luna. "Um, sorry to ask, but will we get those things back at some point?" When Luna lifts her eyebrows in question, I rush to continue. "It's not that I'm against turning them in! Only, I used my allowance to buy some of those things. . . ."

Luna nods. "You'll get everything back at the end of our session, I promise. Until then, we will keep these safe and sound. We're also providing you with Camp Sylvania–approved products so you don't go without." Birdie places a basket of new toiletries on Claire's desk. Luna turns to Claire. "And is there anything you would like to turn in, Claire?"

"Nope," Claire says, the *p* popping loudly. Her arms remain crossed, and she looks beyond annoyed. Mami would absolutely ground me if she saw me making that face at any adult, let alone the camp director . . . if she were also my mom! I'd basically be triple grounded.

But Claire is totally unfazed. It wouldn't surprise me if she and her mom have had a version of this conversation more than once.

Birdie puts her hands on her hips. "Are you sure about that?"

"Are you calling me a liar?" Claire challenges.

Luna lets out a sigh like a gentle breeze. "Lift the mattress, Birdie."

In an instant, Claire's mattress is in the air. Beneath it, clear as day, is a hard-back makeup case.

Luna bends to open the case, which I can see is well-stocked with makeup, lipstick, and hair dye. The kit is neatly organized, and I can tell it's something Claire loves. Who wouldn't?

At the sight of it, Luna tsks loudly, shaking her head. Her long hair sways back and forth, as if every strand is equally as disappointed as she is.

"Now, *this* horrifying display of unnatural products is a clear violation of camp rules. We can't have that," she announces. "And since it comes on the heels of a lie . . ."

All at once, Luna turns the case over and its contents dump out onto the floor like they're garbage, some of the makeup palettes cracking open in the process. I can't help it;

I gasp. The move feels so unnecessary and mean.

Luna continues. "As you know, we will not tolerate this behavior. Birdie?"

Without another word, Birdie grabs the broom from the corner of our room and sweeps the broken cosmetics into a dustpan, tossing them in a nearly full trash bag. I guess they've been collecting a lot of secret contraband during this surprise visit.

My eyes dart to Claire. I'm expecting her to be on the verge of screaming or sobbing, maybe both.

Instead, a calm smile is on Claire's face.

"Why must things always go this way with you?" Luna asks.

Claire simply shrugs.

Luna turns toward me and gently puts her hands on both my shoulders. "I'm so sorry you had to see that. You, dear Nora, have done a wonderful job of being open and honest with us today. We thank you for that." She motions toward the trash bag. "This may seem harsh, but I want you to know that we are only doing this because the chemicals in them are awful for you. I should know. When I was a baby, I was terribly sick from chemicals just like them." Her eyes grow misty as she speaks. "I suffered from severe allergies that kept me from having a normal childhood. I once suffered such a serious reaction to suntan lotion that I ended up hospitalized. I still remember the bright lights and the smell of rubbing alcohol, which to this day makes me feel ill." She sniffles. "So I do all of this, as extreme as it may seem, because I *care*. Please remember that."

Hearing Luna open up this way really makes me feel for her. Even though I don't necessarily agree that outlawing everything synthetic is the way to go, I sort of get it. She's concerned about her campers, yes, but this is also about how Luna's own childhood experience makes her fiercely (and, yeah, excessively . . .) protective of her daughter.

Luna gives one final look around the cabin. "I think we're all set here, Birdie." The iciness in her expression suddenly melts as she gives us a comforting smile. "The bunk really does look lovely, though, girls."

She turns on her heel and heads for the door, Birdie in tow.

As soon as the door shuts behind them, I turn to Claire. "Jeez. That was so intense! How were you so calm?"

I'm thinking about my own mom. I've had huge melt-downs over *way* less, especially these last couple of months navigating the addition of Stepdad Steve and Darren into our home. Yet Claire seems perfectly chill watching some of her favorite items be destroyed by her own mother. At least now I know why there are no photos of her with Luna.

Claire lets out a hollow laugh. "I've gotten used to fights like that with my mom, so it doesn't bother me. I don't let it. I *can't*." Claire reaches into the sleeve of her top and pulls out a sleek tube of bright purple lipstick. "Plus, Mom doesn't know all my secret hiding places."

She opens the lipstick and applies it perfectly, despite not even looking in the mirror.

I'm in total awe, and about to say so, when the two of us hear a scream that sounds like it's coming from the boys' side of camp.

CHAPTER SEVEN
Maggie

As I step outside to pick up the crystals we left to supposedly soak in the moonlight, I notice a traffic jam ahead. Campers have crowded around a cabin at the top of the hill. Without a second thought, I abandon the crystals and head up the path.

"It looks like an animal tore through it," a girl says as I work my way past the swarm of people until I'm standing in front of the cabin called Waning Gibbous.

"Whoa," I whisper as I get a glimpse of the shredded screen windows. One bed is even toppled over with the mattress on the ground in fluffy pieces. Maybe it's just because the cabins are old, but I even notice deep divots in the floor, like someone accidentally scratched or even clawed at the wood. "What the heck happened here?"

"Maggie!" Logan calls as he runs right toward me.

I glance back at the cabin and . . . "Oh my gosh! Logan, this is your cabin! Are you okay?"

"I'm fine," he says, but his eyes are wild with panic and he's breathing heavier than normal. "But I can't find Jesse."

"What? Are you serious? How did you lose *another* bunkmate?"

He looks stricken as he crosses his arms.

"I'm sorry! I didn't mean it like that. Hudson disappearing last summer was definitely not your fault. And besides, Jesse probably just got up early."

"I've lived next door to Jess for six years and I'm pretty sure he has never gotten up early a day in his life without being forcibly removed from his bed."

"I like his style," I mumble. "What about your other bunkmate?"

"He never showed up. Something about surprise summer school, so it was just me and Jesse."

"This place is *not* safe," says a girl behind us named Brooke who I recognize from last summer.

"I told my parents I hated the wilderness," laments a boy with those transition eyeglasses that turn into sunglasses outside. "But they told me not to knock it until I tried it."

"Well, I think it's safe to knock it," another boy responds.

And then I think I even hear someone quietly crying.

"Attention, campers," Luna says as she hustles down the path in her flowy dress with Birdie following behind with two huge trash bags in hand. "No need to panic! It's not good for the nervous system."

Nora squeezes in beside me with Claire just behind her.

"Sort of hard not to panic when my bunkmate is missing," Logan tells Luna.

"Logan, right?" Luna asks.

He nods.

"I was just coming to speak with you. Jesse actually had a family emergency back home. We just sent a counselor with him to the airport, didn't we?" Luna turns to Captain B, who nods with a frown. "Jesse was so sad to go home but knew he needed to be there for his family."

"I hope everything's okay," Nora says.

"One less camper who has to suffer through my mom's hokey nonsense," Claire mumbles. "Besides he seemed as miserable here as I am."

I glance at Claire over my shoulder. How would she even know? Jesse hardly seemed miserable yesterday.

Nora nods along with her, and that just irks me, but I don't say anything to her. Instead, I ask Luna, "How do you explain the totally destroyed cabin? Because to me, it looks like someone or some*thing* went berserk, attacked Jesse, and kidnapped him. Or worse . . ."

Behind me, campers begin to rumble with their own theories.

Luna laughs, and it sounds so natural. It's the kind of laugh you want to join in with, because it's so warm and contagious. "If only camp were that exciting, am I right? Alas, the destroyed screens and the messy room are thanks to a family of squirrels that were nesting in Waning Gibbous over the winter. We'd installed new screens a few days ago, but I suppose they came back."

Beside her, Captain B gives her a dreamy look and lets out a little chuckle. "Those squirrels were so cute."

"Is it just me or does Captain B have major heart eyes for Luna?" I whisper.

"Can you not?" Claire asks. "I'd rather not think of anyone having heart eyes for my mom."

"They *would* make a cute couple," Nora agrees, and the little prickling feelings of annoyance immediately dissipate. I knew we were still on the same page for the most part.

"They would," I say.

Claire rolls her eyes. "Can we just not speculate about my mom being a couple with anyone?"

"All I was going to say is that I don't know how much you know about the last camp director, but I'm not really in the habit of trusting camp directors," I tell her.

Logan nods. "Maggie's on to something. I woke up to a destroyed cabin and a missing bunkmate. Something about that isn't right and I'm pretty sure it's not because of some disgruntled squirrels."

Claire bristles. "I'm not really in the habit of sticking up for my mom, but squirrels are super territorial. And people get homesick at camp all the time."

We all look to Nora, who's been suspiciously silent.

"Let's get some breakfast," she says with a shrug. "I heard

someone say something about waffles."

My stomach growls. Yeah, I know I have a mystery to solve, but my sleuthing skills are no good on an empty stomach.

So it turns out the waffles are made of flaxseed and something about them makes them a little grainy. But compared to the cafeteria offerings last summer, this is basically culinary magic in action and the all-natural maple syrup is pretty great too.

Logan and I sit across from Claire and Nora. I tried talking to Nora when we first sat down, but the cafeteria is so loud we couldn't hear each other, so Logan and I have been replaying the events of this morning and hypothesizing what could be lurking in the shadows this time around.

"What if it's zombies?" he asks.

"Okay, that is actually my worst fear," I say, leaning in excitedly. "But why would they take Jesse and not you? Last time I checked, zombies weren't very picky."

He nods to himself and pushes a syrup-soaked blueberry around his plate. "It just doesn't sit right with me."

"We'll start investigating this afternoon during free time. I knew I would need all the supplies I packed."

"There's not really anything to investigate," Nora says. "It's sad that Jesse went home because of a family emergency, but it sounds like he's okay."

What is she even saying? She can't be for real. How could she even hear us over the noise?

I suddenly realize that campers have started to trickle

out and it's not nearly as loud in here as it was when we first sat down.

"You heard what my mom said," Claire says matter-of-factly. "And we are in the middle of the wilderness, so it's not so unusual for a family of squirrels to go on a rampage in a cabin."

Nora studies her plate and doesn't chime in.

"There's something going on here," I say. "And I'm willing to bet it's paranormal. Come with us, Nora. We're just going to do a little digging around after lunch. Totally safe and above board. Maybe I can even pull Evelyn and Kit away from the chicken coop."

Claire nudges Nora's side. "Or you could come with me to swim. I heard the guys from Full Moon mention hanging out at the lake." She points to a cluster of tall boys with very cool sneakers. They're the kind of boys who run in a pack and always say the most inappropriate things in class but never get in trouble, which I find so frustrating even if most girls swoon over them. "And they're cuuuuuuute."

Nora looks to Claire and then me. "I think I'll go to the lake. You have Logan and this way Claire doesn't have to go alone."

I'm quiet for a moment, waiting for her to change her mind or say she'll catch up with us later to do some investigating herself, but she does neither. Nora never chooses me second, and it hurts like a bruise you can't see but can definitely feel.

"Cool," I finally manage to say. "I can catch you up on our findings later."

She nods noncommittally. "Sure. Yeah. We better head over to our cabin to get changed. I wanna try the moon-water sunscreen."

Claire stands with her tray and Nora follows, leaving me, Logan, our mostly demolished waffles, and a whole ton of unanswered questions.

I feel guilty for being a little excited that suddenly there's a mystery to solve, especially since it involves another missing camper, but I just can't get over the fact that Nora would rather ignore what's right there in front of her face. How can she think about swimming and boys when a camper's life just might be on the line?

I drag my fork through a pool of syrup, trying to bite back the feelings gnawing away at my insides. Maybe Nora and I are just having a bad day. That could be it, right? I hope so. Because that intuition I feel in my gut—the one Dad says never leads him astray—has me thinking that this could be more than a fluke.

This was supposed to be the ultimate summer. Nora's and my big do-over. But not only are campers disappearing again, so is any hope for our perfect summer at sleepaway camp. When did the easiest thing in my life—being best friends with Nora—get so hard?

CHAPTER EIGHT

Nora

I would like to forget all about the slashed window screens at Logan's cabin, and the fact that Jesse is suddenly gone. (Gone, like, POOF! As if he never existed!) I know Luna says he had a family emergency, but would he really go without telling anybody? Not even Logan?

I have little time to process this, though, because after lunch Claire and I need to head to one of these three workshops: Yawning and You, Care and Keeping of Crystals, and Water Has Feelings Too! (which is apparently based on a real book).

"I can't take that last workshop seriously," I say, sideeyeing the chalkboard where the classes are listed. "I feel bad enough if I don't give my favorite outfits equal attention. If I have to start sympathizing with water, I'll never get anything done!"

"We're absolutely not doing that one," Claire assures me. "I signed us up for Yawning and You. I'm hoping it means we can lie down and take a nap."

I grin. "Now, *that* I can get behind."

She and I make our way into a meditation space. There are cozy pillows and lush plants everywhere. Blackout curtains remove most of the light except for a collection of fake, flickering candles displayed around the room.

Luna sits cross-legged on a tufted green cushion at the head of the room. Her eyes are closed as campers enter.

Claire groans beside me. "I didn't know *she'd* be teaching this class. Let's bail!" She starts to leave, but I grab her arm.

"What? No! Yawning and You was your idea." I point toward two pillows near the door. "Come on. It's dark. If we sit at the back, she probably won't even notice us."

"Doubtful." Claire huffs as she plops down.

"Welcome, welcome," Luna's voice murmurs from the front of the room. "Make yourselves comfortable. Kick off your shoes. Settle in."

She keeps her eyes closed and takes in a long breath. She does this a few times as if she's in no rush while the rest of us stare awkwardly at her.

"Yawning is something we all do, yet few of us do it well," Luna begins. "This reflex is our body's way of letting us know we are tired, stressed, bored, or even hungry. It is the way our bodies tell us: 'Pay attention to me.' Today, I will teach you how to best maximize your yawns so that you may respond to your body and let it know, 'I am listening.'"

Claire snorts. "Who knew my mother could turn simple

70

body functions into something so dramatic?"

I hold in a laugh and shake my head. "Let's just hope she lets us lie down."

"I'm not waiting for permission," Claire says, flopping back and snuggling into a pillow.

"To begin, a yawn has three phases: first is a gradual mouth gaping as you breathe in, which is followed by a brief period of muscle stretching, and ends with a muscle relaxation as you expel the air. Let me demonstrate." Luna tilts her head back and opens her mouth so wide she looks like Kirby, the video game character. Then her shoulders drop as she emits a wail so loud several campers in the class visibly jump.

"Was that necessary?" JJ Richardson, who is giving off some big too-cool-for-pretty-much-everything vibes, asks from the front of the class.

"Seriously," Claire mutters.

Luna finally opens her eyes and gives him a small smile. "When yawning the correct way, it is necessary to tilt your head back and allow one's mouth to hang open, then to take in a deep breath and let your shoulders relax. When the yawn comes, as it did for me, you can stretch your jaw muscles and your whole body and lean into it. For me, this is best done with a primal yell. For you, it may be different. Thank you for the excellent question! Are there any others?"

When no one speaks, Luna closes her eyes once more. "For the rest of class, we will practice this yawning technique together, and I encourage you to really feel it. Here we go.

Close your eyes. Tilt your head back. Allow your mouth to hang open widely."

I look over at Claire. But instead of closing my eyes, I cross them. Then I tilt my head back, open my mouth, and stick my tongue out the side so I probably resemble a dead fish. She laughs.

"Breathe deeply," Luna instructs.

I do.

"Now, exhale and, if it feels right, shout . . ."

Expecting the class to follow Luna's lead with the yelp, I let out a silly "Ahhhhhh"—only to realize I'm the only one! All the campers turn to look at me while Claire hides behind her pillow, laughing hysterically. I'm really regretting not escaping this workshop when Claire gave me the chance.

Luna claps her hands together excitedly. "Impressive! Who was that? Please stand."

"It's really nothing. . . ." I reply meekly.

"Nonsense! You've risen to the challenge. Stand!"

Reluctantly, I get to my feet, feeling like my whole face is on fire. Maybe if I'm lucky the ground will decide now's a good time to open up and I can be swallowed whole.

"Oh! Is that Nova?" Luna asks, misremembering my name.

"It's, um, Nora," I say.

"Nora!" Luna claps again. "You, my dear, are today's star pupil. Everyone, let's follow Nora's example and try again. Don't be afraid to let go!"

I receive a few dirty looks (which I probably deserve) as I sit down, absolutely mortified. Claire is practically crying from holding in her laughter.

"Get it together," I hiss at her.

"Can't. Won't. Refuse to," she manages between stifled giggles.

By now, the class is ready to exhale, and I can see Luna motion toward me encouragingly. I have no choice but to offer another yell!

This time, though, Claire joins me. "AHHHHHHH!" she screams from next to me, and between that sound as well as the half-hearted shouts from the other campers, the whole class devolves into laughter.

"Yes!" Luna cheers. "Laughter can be part of the release! Lean into it! Okay, again . . ."

By the time we've finished, I hate to admit that Yawning and You was actually kind of fun. Even though Luna's prompts were totally ridiculous, it was nice to let loose like that, especially after this morning's scare with the shredded windows.

I go from giggly to nervous in a matter of moments as I head down to the lake to hang out with Claire and the boys from the Full Moon cabin.

Confession: I have never been alone with boys who aren't my brothers. And let's be real, my brothers are like 99 percent nuisance and only 1 percent boy.

So I'm nervous. What do I say? What do I do? Is my outfit okay? What if they don't like me? What if I don't like *them*?

I don't know.

What I do know is that I'll need to put on the performance of a lifetime at the lake so nobody notices how anxious I'm feeling. (Never mind that I'm not convinced this new "crystal deodorant" from Luna actually works. When Claire's not looking, I take a quick moment to sniff my armpit and make sure I don't stink. All clear.)

At the shore of the lake, Big Liam, who has floppy blond hair and blue eyes, is whooping and hollering as he splashes his friends, Elijah and another boy with deep dimples and neon green braces. They're not in their bathing suits, so everyone's regular clothes are getting drenched.

"Dude, I wish we had my squirt guns," the boy with braces says as he splashes back at Big Liam. "I can't believe Loopy Luna confiscated them."

Loopy Luna? Yikes.

I steal a glance over at Claire, but she laughs.

"Of *course* my mom did that, and I'm sure she gave some silly reason, like, 'Squirt guns don't align with your chi.'"

Big Liam quits splashing the others and his eyebrows shoot up. "Wait. Loopy Luna's your mom?"

"Unfortunately," Claire says with an eye roll.

"No way!" Elijah shakes his head. "That must kinda suck. No offense."

"It's cool. At least it means that Nora and I get our own cabin. Right, Nora?" Claire gives me an encouraging nod.

"Oh, yeah," I agree. "It's practically our own little house."

That's a complete exaggeration, but the boy without a name—who I'm choosing to call Dimples—nods in approval. "Nice."

There's a second of awkward silence. I wish I could think of something interesting to say.

Big Liam beats me to it. "I dare one of you to run into the lake right now."

"No way, man." Elijah shakes his head. "We'll get in trouble. You know we're not supposed to swim without one of the counselors watching."

"You scared?" Big Liam starts bawking and jerking his head back and forth like a chicken. Why is his chicken impression kinda good?

"I'll do it!" Claire announces.

Without another word, she kicks off her shoes and splashes into the water all the way up to her waist.

"Dude! She went for it!" Big Liam puts his fist up to his mouth, laughing, as the others cheer.

A shrill whistle blows from behind us. We turn to see Captain B, hands on her hips. "You five: Step away from the lake!"

Busted.

Because of Claire's lake stunt, Captain B makes us all turn in early that night as punishment—no campfire, no dessert, no free time.

Claire is totally unfazed, though, and I'm buzzing from

the adrenaline of it all. I've never been a rule breaker before, but it was sort of thrilling. Plus, it seems like Maggie is getting in even deeper with her paranormal obsession, and I have to admit it's kind of nice having my own thing, something that feels *normal*.

"I can't believe you ran into the lake!" I flop back onto my bed dramatically. "So awesome!"

Claire grins at me, pulling off her wet (and now seriously dirt-caked) socks and tossing them in with her dirty laundry. "I couldn't pass up a dare."

"The only dare I've ever done was watch an R-rated movie after my mom told me not to." I sigh. "I had nightmares for weeks."

Claire laughs. "You're adorable. And I need to change out of these clothes . . . but what do you say we skip tomorrow's morning workshop sessions and head to the abandoned boathouse?"

I make a face. "The abandoned boathouse? Why?"

She gives me a shrug. "Because Big Liam invited us."

I feel a smile spread across my face. "Wait, really?"

"Really. You're in, right?"

I give her a firm nod. "I'm in."

That's how I find myself ditching class (a first!) and hanging out with Claire and the boys for the second time in twenty-four hours. Maybe some of Claire's easygoing vibes are rubbing off on me!

"How much do you wanna bet the abandoned boathouse is haunted?" Claire says nonchalantly. "I mean, I never did find out why my mom roped it off. . . ."

"Don't even joke," I groan. "I'm nervous enough as it is!"

Claire eyes me. "Nervous? Why?"

Do I tell her I've been a little jumpy because the supernatural and I are not exactly besties, or do I openly admit I'm a complete novice in the crush department? The second option actually sounds less embarrassing.

"Oh, um. Just because the boys seem really cool."

Claire bumps her shoulder into mine. "Ooh, you like them! Which one? Is it Elijah?" I look away, and Claire squeals. "I knew it! You think Elijah's cute!"

"Shh, not so loud!" I whisper, looking around. "What if someone hears you?"

"I hope they do. Then I can play matchmaker," she teases.

I bite back a smile. "So, do you really not know why the boathouse has been closed?"

Claire waves a hand in the air. "Oh, yeah. Mom said letting campers take boats out on the lake was a total liability."

I wrinkle my brows in confusion. "But the blob is somehow fine?"

"Don't try to figure Luna out," Claire warns. "Trust me. I've tried, and it'll give you a headache."

"Fine. I was just thinking it might have been fun to take a boat out onto the water."

"Yeah, but now we get to sneak into the boathouse with

some boys. *Cute* boys," Claire reminds me. "Apparently they found a vintage stereo and Big Liam's obsessed."

"Seriously? What a throwback."

"I know, right?" With a laugh, Claire leads the way into the boathouse, where Big Liam, Elijah, and Dimples (we really gotta find out that kid's name . . .) are throwing rocks at some of the overturned boats.

"We heard there's a rock party?" The boys look up at us. "Get it? *Rock* party?" Claire motions toward the rock in Elijah's hand.

He laughs. "That's good."

"Thanks!" She beams. "Sorry I got you guys banished to your bunk early last night."

Big Liam pushes his floppy hair out of his face, and I find myself thinking he looks like he could be in one of those old boy bands my mom still swoons over. "It's all good. It's not like we wanted to be part of whatever touchy-feely thing was happening by the campfire anyway."

"At breakfast, I overheard Sara Park saying the counselors changed the lyrics to the Hokey Pokey song and made it all about sharing your feelings." I shudder. "Can you imagine?"

"Now, that's just sad," Elijah says, shaking his head.

Claire points toward a silver object at the back of the boathouse. "Is that the stereo?"

"It is. Come see!" Dimples motions us over. "It's huge, right?"

Compared to our phones, it really is, even though it's no

bigger than Maggie's dog, Pickle. But I can't imagine having to lug a big stereo around just to be able to listen to music.

The stereo is sleek and silver, with a handle on top. It's in pretty good shape except for a couple of scratches on the body. The rounded black speakers remind me of giant bug eyes. If Maggie were here, we'd probably giggle over how the whole thing looks like a baby alien, but I realize this seems like a pretty kiddish thought to have, so I keep it to myself.

"My mom says everyone had one of these when she was our age." Big Liam taps the top of the stereo with a familiarity that makes me think maybe he was the one to find it. "Apparently there were even bigger ones than this, with huge speakers and all! This one's portable so you can either plug it in or use batteries to bring it wherever. See? It's not even heavy." He swoops down to lift the stereo with just one finger to show us.

"Does it work?" I ask.

Elijah nods, reaching for a CD sitting in a stack next to the boom box. The cover features distressed red-and-black lettering that reads: AMERICAN IDIOT. "Check it out."

A dramatic voice roars from the speaker, *"Don't wanna be an American idiot!"* followed by explosive guitar riffs.

Elijah silently mouths the lyrics as he listens. Then he looks between Claire and me. "Good, huh?"

"It's awesome!" Claire gushes. She nudges me. "Right, Nora?"

"Right," I agree, even though the music is not really my taste. "Who is it?"

"Green Day," Big Liam says. "They were, like, huge back in the day."

"I wish they were big now! Can you just imagine hearing this live?" Claire bobs her head along with the song, her blue hair catching the sun as she does, and she hums along, already catching on to the beat. How does she always look so effortlessly cool? And know the right thing to say? I've never even been to a concert, unless the Wiggles count.

Clearing my throat, I look over at Dimples. "Hey, so, um, what did you say your name was again?"

He puffs out his chest. "Big Liam."

Claire's brows furrow and she points at the kid we already know as Big Liam. "Wait. I thought he was Big Liam."

"I am!" He slings his arm around Dimples's shoulders. "We're *both* Big Liam."

"How exactly did that happen?" Claire asks with a laugh.

Dimples shrugs. "Well, we're both named Liam, so we tried to come up with a way for people to remember who's who. I wanted to be called Big Liam first—"

Big Liam interrupts. "But I said if there's only *one* Big Liam, it implies the other one's small. Which I'm not. We're both the same height *and* we can do the same number of push-ups."

Elijah shakes his head, quietly adding, "Yet I can do the most push-ups out of all of us."

Dimples scowls at him. "Doubtful."

"You couldn't even lift a bowling ball, let alone yourself,"

Big Liam teases, giving Elijah a playful shove.

"I can prove it," Elijah says. "Push-up challenge?"

Big Liam grabs Elijah and puts him in a headlock, and Dimples joins in. All three of them start to wrestle and I suddenly feel like I'm watching my older brothers roughhouse in my living room.

Maybe these guys aren't as mature as I thought.

"I'm clearly the strongest!" Big Liam announces. "Say it! Say I'm the strongest!"

Elijah wiggles out from under his grip. "Whatever, man. I'm the one who could easily take down whatever destroyed that cabin earlier."

"You want to fight a family of squirrels?" Claire teases.

Dimples's eyebrows go up. "Is that what it was? Here I was thinking it was a bear or something."

"It was definitely a wolf," Big Liam confirms. "Maybe even—"

"Hey, don't scare them!" Dimples cuts him off. "You have nothing to worry about. We'll keep you safe." He winks at Claire.

"Yeah. We're like our own little wolf pack," Elijah assures us. "We've got this."

Big Liam cups his hands around his mouth and lets out a loud *ah*-OOOOOooOOOO in his best attempt at a wolf howl. Dimples and Elijah join in.

Claire claps her hands together, commanding their attention. "Let's play two truths and a lie! Come on."

The boys immediately stop howling and follow her over to an old canoe, where they all take seats, arguing over who should go first. They roughhouse a little more as they do. I can tell they're trying to show off, trying to impress Claire. Even though she's my friend, I'm a little jealous of how easily she holds their interest.

"Okay, okay, okay." Dimples tries to quiet his friends down. "I'm going first. I've never tried soda. I'm a triplet. And I can play guitar."

"Man, no way you've never tried soda," Elijah says.

Big Liam nods in agreement. "Seriously, dude. What are you, an alien?"

"I'm going with triplet as the lie," Claire says. "The world can't handle *four* cute Big Liams walking around!"

Both Liams flush at this.

Elijah just shakes his head, but the way he sneaks glances at Claire makes me wonder if he wishes she were flirting with him instead of the Liams. Does anyone even care that I'm here?

"Um," I pipe up. "I guess I'll say soda too."

"Drumroll, please . . . ," Dimples says, as Elijah and Big Liam drum their hands on their legs. "All right, I'm definitely *not* a triplet."

Claire slaps her knee. "I knew it!"

"Yeah, so you're an alien, then," Elijah says. "Because no soda? Ever?!"

"My mom's a health nut," Dimples explains. "Carbonated

drinks are banned from our house!"

"You've never even taken a sip?" Elijah asks.

"Nope!"

"You gotta. Soda is the fizzy nectar of the gods!" Big Liam insists, and the group bursts out laughing, so I laugh along, too, even though I don't find it all *that* funny.

"You sound like a commercial," Claire teases, which makes Big Liam repeat himself, and everyone's laughing even harder.

A loud scream suddenly grabs my attention—yet Claire and the boys don't even seem to hear it over their laughter—and I jerk my head toward the sound. Through one of the propped-open windows, I can make out a circle of campers sitting with Birdie. Right. At breakfast, Maggie told me she and Logan would be at their Primal Screaming 101 workshop.

I scan the circle for their familiar faces. My heart sinks a little when I spot them, seated beside one another, whispering and laughing like they're in on a secret. A part of me wishes *I* was the one sitting next to Maggie whispering and laughing, like old times, instead of being here, feeling awkward.

"Helloooo?" Claire's voice snaps me back to the present. "Earth to Nora?"

"Sorry! What'd I miss?" I ask.

"Big Liam's about to go next." She points at Big Liam. "Go for it."

"Okay." Big Liam holds up a new finger each time he lists a statement off. "One: I can hold my breath underwater for one minute. Two: I'm really into working out. Three: I have supersonic hearing."

"Supersonic hearing," Claire and Dimples say at the same time, before yelling, "Jinx!"

"Definitely supersonic hearing." I wrinkle my nose. "Is that even a thing?"

"Nah, it's the workout one. Because if you were really into working out, you'd have agreed to the push-up challenge earlier," Elijah teases.

Big Liam shakes his head. "You're all wrong. I can actually hold my breath underwater for *two* minutes, so that was the lie."

"You have really good hearing, then?" Claire asks.

"Freakishly good!" He juts out his chin proudly. "I was the one who heard the howling the other night. That's how I know it was definitely a wolf that attacked that cabin."

"Wait, really?" I ask. "You actually heard a wolf?"

"Sure did. Elijah heard it too."

Elijah offers a half shrug. "I mean, I had to listen really hard to make it out, but yeah. It definitely sounded like howling."

"Like I said, though, we'll keep you safe." Dimples scoots closer to Claire.

"We'll *all* keep you safe," Big Liam chimes in. "Nothing to worry about."

"Oh, I'm not worried," Claire promises. "My turn now!"

As Claire shares her two truths and a lie, I file away what Big Liam just said. I may not be into the whole paranormal investigation thing, but I will definitely be telling Maggie that something *did* attack that cabin, and it wasn't a family of squirrels.

Thank goodness it was only a wolf and not something paranormal.

CHAPTER NINE
Maggie

"Maggie Bananas!" Birdie sings as I shuffle into her morning workshop circle on the main lawn. "And Logan! I'm so glad you're both here. I was getting a little nervous about my attendance numbers for Primal Screaming 101."

A quick glance around and it's clear that Birdie's not totally wrong to be a little worried.

"Wouldn't miss it for the world, Captain B," Logan tells her.

What we don't say is that Logan and I tried to get into Foraging for Mother Nature's Pharmacy and Meditative Finger Painting only to find out they were already full. It's not that I don't want to hang out with Birdie. It's just that nothing—and I mean *nothing*—about primal screaming interests me. I don't even like having to go to the bathroom in the middle of a class and drawing attention to myself. Why would I want to scream my head off with all eyes on me?

Last Summer Maggie would have been all about primal

screaming (whatever that is) and would have happily stepped into the limelight. But This Summer Maggie is a whole new girl and she's all about the secrets of the paranormal world around her and less about belting her guts out in front of other campers.

Logan and I take a seat in the circle on one of the cushions that look like they came straight from the renaissance festival Dad took me and Nora to over spring break. (He said it was official research for his new book series about time-traveling knights, but I think he just actually liked walking around with a fake sword on his hip.)

Other glum-looking campers begin to gather who also seem to have been turned away from the more enticing activities like digging for fossils on the shore, making face masks out of blueberries, and decorating gratitude journals.

Birdie clears her throat as she paces the outside of the circle. "Well, I guess we better get started," she says, sounding almost a little nervous.

"Is it too late to sneak away?" I whisper to Logan as I wonder if Nora and Claire really went off to the old boathouse. It's not like Nora to skip . . . anything. One time, her mom offered to take us out of school early to see a movie and Nora told her she didn't want to ruin her attendance record.

"I really want to get out into the woods and see if we can find any more clues," Logan says. "Luna's story about Jesse just doesn't check out for me." Our clue hunting expedition yesterday afternoon wasn't all that successful. Although, we did find a stockpile of acorns in his cabin, and I did retrieve my acne cream, thank God.

"Has anyone heard of primal screaming?" Birdie asks.

No one answers out loud, but one girl meekly raises her hand.

"I wonder if we're dealing with faeries here," I whisper. "From what I've read, they're as vicious as they are beautiful."

Logan's eyes widen. "Oh man, that would be wild. What about some kind of creature though? Like . . . like a Big Foot!"

"Primal screaming is one of those things that is so wonderfully simple it can feel complicated," Birdie says. "Personally, I only started practicing primal screaming a few months ago after Luna shared it with me. It really helped me get over some . . . sister issues. She really knows how to suck the life out of you if you get what I mean." She chuckles to herself. "It's not as simple as pulling each other's ponytails like when we were kids, ya know? Anyway, primal scream-ing has already become my favorite part of the day, and when you live out in the woods like I do, there's no one around to bother so we can really let loose out here."

I laugh under my breath. "I'm sure my dad would really love waking up to my morning primal scream before I brush my teeth."

"Yeah, that wouldn't be cause for concern," Logan agrees.

"This circle should feel like a safe space," Birdie contin-ues. "Letting your inner scream out is a way for you to process past trauma. Rage, even. And, eventually, it will remind you of all the strength inside of you that's been there all along."

I don't want to say it out loud . . . but all this talk about primal screaming makes Birdie sound a little like she's been brainwashed. Considering the googly eyes she's been making at Luna since we got here, it makes me a little nervous that maybe Captain B isn't really seeing things for what they are. Between this, the trashed cabin yesterday morning, and Luna's hokey moon water, I'm pretty sure things aren't quite right at Camp Sylvania.

"The best way to do it is to try it," she says, "so let's take turns giving it our best shot."

A younger, but very smug-looking boy across the circle raises his hand. "Maybe you could give us an example of your primal scream first, Miss Captain B."

Birdie shrugs and nods before taking three huge huffing breaths in and out and in and out and in and out. And then a sound like nothing I've ever heard rips through her chest as she flings her arms out wide, like she's daring the universe to just try to mess with her.

Except the actual noise Birdie makes sounds less like a scream and more like . . . a croak.

"Whoa," I whisper.

"Okay, your turn," Birdie tells the boy.

The boy's face is bright red as he tries his best not to laugh.

"Not to primal scream shame . . . ," Logan says as the boy screams.

"But Captain B sounded like a dying horse," I finish.

He shakes his head. "I was going to say an angry seal, but I guess I can see the horse thing."

"Speaking of dead horses . . . I wonder if the woods are infested with angry ghost animals. Like maybe some ghost bear tore through the cabin looking for her cubs."

Logan frowns. "Okay, that's, like, super sad."

"And seeing Howie frozen in time isn't super sad?"

"Well, that's different. He wears a tie-dye shirt. And he went out doing what he loved, right? Jet Skiing."

I nod and then flinch as another camper squawks out a primal scream.

I really should have brought the earplugs Mom packed for this session.

A pair of lavender Jordans catch my eye on a girl three cushions down. Dang. Nora would fuh-reak out for those sneakers. She even has these really cool pink-and-blue reflective heart decals that remind me of Nora's favorite Taylor Swift album. (*Lover*, of course. I'm a *Red* girl myself.) I need to track down Nora after this to tell her about this girl's shoes.

Glancing over my shoulder, I look around like she might suddenly decide she'd rather hang out with me, but all I see is more trees and all I hear is another ear-splitting scream.

"Maggie," Birdie says. "Are you with us?"

My back straightens at the sound of her using my name without the word *Bananas* attached. It feels like when Mom calls me by my full name, Magnolia.

"You're up," Birdie says, and waves her hand for me to stand. "Show us what you got."

My legs wobble as I get up and feel all eyes on me, including Logan's.

And suddenly I'm back on that stage last summer facing off with Sylvia. Except then, I had Nora by my side. Now I just have a bunch of tweens staring back at me and my bestie is nowhere to be found.

Here goes nothing.

I open my mouth and let loose, but all that comes out is a half-hearted "Ahhhhhhhhh," like someone's just snuck up on me but I saw them coming the whole time. Like this is all one big joke and I could never possibly take it seriously.

A couple of kids laugh, but not in a mean way. More like in a this-is-silly-and-it's-cool-not-to-care kind of way. And I hate to admit that I like how it feels, so I laugh a little too and then let out an even more monotone scream before taking a bow and sitting down.

"Nice artistic choice," Logan whispers.

I bite down on my lip to keep myself from smiling too hard and losing all the cool points I just gained.

Birdie crosses her arms. "Huh. Maggie, something tells me you're not putting your best scream forward." She starts to pace the circle again and I can't believe she's singling me out. "The whole purpose of this exercise is to get out of your own head, people. Be free. Embrace that part of yourself that wants to scream when you're angry or sad or excited. Let it all out. Don't cheat yourself of this experience."

She turns back and our eyes connect.

And I guess she's right. When I opened my mouth, I really did mean to let go, but that's not what came out. It's just a silly scream though. Surely, it doesn't matter.

Right?

Beside me, Logan stands with his hands on his hips. He closes his eyes and inhales deeply through his nose before letting out the most ferocious scream we've heard yet.

"Now, that's what I call primal!" Birdie yells with a hoot.

The other campers nod and a few even clap. The guy next to Logan with shaggy hair says, "So metal."

"Impressive," I tell him as he plops back down.

"My dad's big into screamo bands, so between that and musical theater, my lung capacity is pretty major." He pauses for a minute, his fingers tugging up pieces of grass. "And it did feel kinda good. I've been feeling pretty tense all day with Jesse leaving so soon."

"I'm—I'm glad," I finally say.

"You should give it a real go," he tells me.

I nod a little too aggressively. "Yeah. For sure."

Thankfully, our time runs out before the circle gets back to me.

A bugle-like sound rings through the camp-wide speaker system, letting us know that it's officially free time.

I'm feeling a little guilty over my jokey scream, so I

head over to Birdie to apologize with Logan just a few steps behind me.

"Captain B," I call just as another voice calls, "Birdie! Could I see you in my cabin?"

I wind past a crowd of girls making afternoon plans to find Luna beckoning Birdie and Birdie dutifully following her back up the hill.

"Something's definitely up with those two," Logan says.

"You know what I'm thinking?" I say as any remaining feelings of guilt melt away. "If anyone knows what the deal is with Luna, it's Birdie."

"So you're saying we should spy on the one adult who sided with us to defeat her vampire sister last summer?" he asks.

I hate to admit it, but . . . "I guess I am."

"Adults," Logan says with a sigh. "You can't even trust the good ones."

CHAPTER TEN
Nora

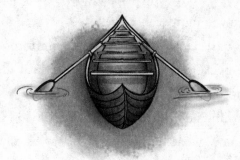

Before this afternoon, I had no idea there was a right and a wrong way to burn sage, or that the practice has Indigenous roots that date back literal centuries. But the Respectful Sage Burning session I attended, led by Luna herself, stressed the importance of being mindful of Indigenous traditions, supporting Native-owned businesses, and using sage purposefully and sparingly.

Now that I understand the intricacies of the practice, I'm rethinking that sage kit I'd bought from Urban Outfitters (which did absolutely nothing to cleanse our house from Stepdad Steve). I even write a letter home to Mami sharing what I learned.

Being taught by Luna definitely gave me a new appreciation for her. She was thoughtful in her approach and I actually learned a ton. Who knew there was more to Camp Sylvania 2.0 than moon water and lavender garlands?

I'm so excited to fill Maggie in on everything that

happened today that I practically race to dinner. After barely seeing her for the past twenty-four hours, I'm dying to tell Maggie about the howling wolf Big Liam heard. Plus, I just know she'll die laughing when I tell her there are *two* Big Liams at camp.

The dining hall is packed when I arrive. After I get my food—magenta-colored ravioli that look more like flower petals than pasta—I worry I won't even find an open seat, let alone my friend. Thankfully, after elbowing my way through the crowd, I spot her near the drink machine and rush over to her yelling, "Magpie!"

Her face breaks into a bright smile when she sees me. "There you are!"

"Gosh, it's a zoo in here tonight, huh?"

"Tell me about it," Maggie says, glancing around. "How are we ever going to find a seat? Also, does it smell sort of funny in here?"

"You mean does it smell like someone took every last stick of deodorant and threw it away? Yeah. The BO is out of control."

"Nora! Maggie!" a familiar voice says from behind us. We turn to see Claire, who is waving at us from a table where she and Logan have claimed ownership of two empty chairs by putting their trays on them. "Over here!"

We hurry to them. I plunk down my tray and let out a sigh of relief. "You're a *lifesaver*."

"Logan's idea," Claire says.

"Glad you guys showed up when you did." Logan juts his chin toward a group of scowling campers. "They look ready to pounce."

"We could totally take them," Maggie jokes, plopping into the chair beside Logan. I grab the seat between her and Claire.

"Anyone know what this is supposed to be?" Logan flares his nostrils in disgust, stabbing a piece of ravioli with his fork.

"Raw beet ravioli stuffed with vegan cashew cheese topped with diced apple and walnuts," Claire chirps in her best Luna impression, before she visibly shudders. "One of Mom's favorites, and one of my *least*. What's wrong with regular ravioli, you know? Even Chef Boyardee would be better."

Maggie cuts in. "What's so bad about Chef Boyardee?"

To which Claire shrugs. "Nothing, really, just not my thing. Then again, neither is this."

And that tension that always seems to be bubbling between Maggie and Claire returns. My stomach twists. I hate how even little things like ravioli cause disagreements between them, as if to prove how different Maggie and Claire really are. At this rate, I worry they'll never get along, and I'll have to spend the whole summer ping-ponging between my two friends.

"Well, I'd kill for some Chef Boyardee right about now." Logan lets his rubbery piece of ravioli fall to his plate. "But can we focus on something else while I force this down?"

I inwardly sigh with relief.

"Nora and I played hooky from this morning's session and ended up going to meet up with those boys at the abandoned boathouse," Claire says. "They really did find a stereo!"

"Did it work?" Logan asks. Then he pinches his nose as he takes a bite of his food.

Maggie blinks. "You really skipped your morning session?"

I feel my cheeks flush. "Just this once," I promise.

"It's not like we'll get in trouble. Privileges of knowing the owner." Claire winks. "And the stereo did work! We even played some old CDs, right, Nora?"

I nod, suddenly wishing Claire hadn't started telling this story. I worry it makes me look shallow and boy obsessed, which is only a *little* true. "We listened to one from a band called Green Bay. Apparently they were a big deal, but they're no Taylor Swift."

Claire laughs. "Green *Day*. I thought you said you liked them?"

Ugh, right, I did say that.

"I mean, they were good, just not what I normally listen to," I explain quickly.

"Maggie!" A voice calls. Grace Byrne, a girl with red hair pulled back into two French braids, jogs over to our table. "Great scream earlier." She lets out a dull *ahhhhhh* and then she, Maggie, and Logan start laughing.

"It was some of my best work," Maggie says with a grin. "Yours was great too, Grace! And my ears are still practically ringing from Logan's."

Grace nods. "It was horror-film good."

Logan does a tiny bow. "Thank you for recognizing my talents. Years of listening to screamo bands and learning how to project in musical theater has finally paid off."

I frown as I watch the exchange. Maybe if I had gone to the Primal Screaming 101 session with Captain B instead of the dumb boathouse, then I could be part of this conversation too.

After Grace leaves, I feel like this is my chance to finally fill Maggie in on what I learned from Big Liam. She needs to know that actual, real wolves are roaming camp!

But as I open my mouth to speak, Maggie beats me to it. "That reminds me!" she says, getting excited. "During Primal Screaming 101, I saw a girl who had a killer pair of lavender Jordans. You would've loved them! They had these amazing little heart decals on the side in pink and blue and it looked just like the cover of *Lover*."

She looks at me like she's waiting for me to gush over the shoes, too, but something inside me deflates like a balloon. We finally get a chance to catch up and Maggie wants to talk about shoes? Is this all my best friend thinks I care about now that I skipped one session and hung out with some boys?

"Those sound cute," I say, trying not to let my disappointment show. But I'm sure Maggie can sense my lack of enthusiasm when her eyebrows knit together in concern.

"Yeah, they were . . . but what was it you wanted to tell me?"

I bite my lower lip. "Oh, um. It's not important. Never mind."

Maggie leans closer to me. "NorBear, I—"

The rest of her sentence is drowned out by Luna's voice ringing out over the camp-wide speaker system.

"Attention, campers! I have an important announcement to make."

Logan elbows Maggie, whispering, "Maybe it'll be about Jesse and the cabin windows."

"Let's hope," she whispers back.

Luna continues. "I'm delighted to share that at the end of the summer session we will be holding Camp Sylvania's first-ever Moon Ball! This will be the perfect way to say farewell to summer and celebrate coming into our most true selves. Dance lessons will be optional. More details will be shared soon. Have a magical evening, campers!"

All at once, the dining hall erupts into excited chatter about the dance.

Claire nudges my shoulder with hers. "You gonna ask Elijah to the Moon Ball?"

"Elijah?" I make a face. "I don't think he liked me very much."

"He was totally checking you out!" she insists.

"Who's Elijah?" Maggie asks.

"Nora's new crush!" Claire teases.

Maggie's face falls. Part of me wants to swoop in to correct Claire and tell Maggie she'd always be the first one to know if I had a new crush. But the other part of me is feeling like I can't say or do anything right today. Would it even matter?

So I say nothing, instead pretending to be extremely invested in Logan's rant about the time he had to take long and intense dance lessons for his older cousin's quinceañera, and how he definitely won't be doing that again, thankyouverymuch.

When we all get up to clear our trays, I use the bustling crowd as an opportunity to slip away from the group unnoticed. Between being completely invisible to the Full Moon boys earlier, not feeling cool enough for Claire, worrying Maggie and I are totally out of sync, and that jealous pang I get whenever I see Maggie and Logan sharing a moment, I could really use some time alone.

I find myself over by the moon-water tub. It's quiet over here, serene, the water glistening under the glow from the night sky.

As much as I don't want to admit it, this unsure feeling I've been dealing with lately is sort of new. The old me had kinda gotten used to being center stage. I had to! I was often performing, and nobody wants to see an actor who's not feeling confident. These new feelings have me wondering if I made the right decision coming back to Camp Sylvania, or if

I should've stayed home and tried summer dance lessons or something. At least then I'd get to put my performance skills to good use.

Even though I'm alone, I let out a sigh.

"I come here to take some time for myself sometimes too. It's peaceful, isn't it?" asks that breezy, gentle voice I've come to know as Luna's. I look up to see her seated on one of the nearby logs, legs folded and hands pressed together as if she was just meditating. The setting sun's rays spill down onto her and the butter-colored gauzy dress she's wearing. I was so caught up in my own thoughts that I hadn't even noticed her there.

"It is," I say with a nod.

"Is everything okay, Nora? You seem sad."

"I'm fine."

"Oh, my dear." She lets out a soft sigh. "Fitting in can be tough sometimes." That admission surprises me even more than Luna remembering my name. What does Luna know about fitting in? She seems like the most confident person in the world, and she raised a daughter who's the same.

I glance down sheepishly. "What gave me away?"

Luna gives me a kind smile. "You're here, alone, after dinner rather than off with your friends during free time. I figured something might be going on."

"Oh. Right." I shift from one foot to another awkwardly. "I kind of snuck off. Just needed some fresh air, I guess."

"We could all use a break from time to time." Luna nods

sagely. "But remember that being true to yourself, especially among friends, is what's most important. Living as your most authentic self is about letting your *own* inner beauty shine."

I sigh. "What if your natural, best self sometimes doesn't feel good enough for other people?"

"Part of being yourself is not worrying about what other people think and still being confident in who you are," Luna says. "For what it's worth, Nora, I can see your inner beauty shining."

I feel the corners of my lips curve up into a smile. How is it that this almost-stranger knew exactly what I needed to hear?

"Really?" I ask softly.

"Really." Luna rises from where she's perched and walks over to me in a way that's so graceful it's almost as if she's floating. She hands me a crystal vial, and from its glow, I can tell it's filled with moon water. "Use a bit of this tonight before bedtime and feel better. Soon, you'll be able to see your inner beauty shining too."

CHAPTER ELEVEN
Maggie

After dinner, Logan and I break off from the group hanging out near the cafeteria. There's some free time before curfew and most people are spending it goofing off in large groups or sneaking off in pairs . . . to be alone. Whatever that means.

I almost stop to explain to Nora where we're going, but she's somehow managed to totally disappear into the crowd of dining hall chaos.

"I'm not actually sure where Captain B's cabin is," I tell Logan. "I honestly thought she lived in the craft barn last year."

"I always saw her going in and out of the woods last summer," he says as we get farther and farther away, and suddenly the laughter is drowned out by the buzzing of cicadas as the sun sinks past the horizon.

Instinctively, my hand flies to my pocket to make sure my mini flashlight is there, though I wish we had stopped at my cabin for my bag of remaining supplies that weren't confiscated by Luna. There's no telling who or what we might encounter in the woods.

Except we don't have to go far at all before stumbling across a little log cabin with twinkle lights strung up across the porch. Captain B sits with her legs crossed and some kind of rocks balanced on her knees with candles and crystals surrounding her.

"There it is!" I say just in time for Logan to yank me back behind a tree.

"Whoa," I whisper. "I thought we were here to ask Captain B about Luna."

"We were until we found her meditating on her porch in a circle of crystals."

"Uhhhh, maybe she's just researching," I offer. "Like how she became a slayer last summer."

Logan shakes his head. "Or she dove headfirst into whatever gimmicky thing Luna's got going on and she can't be trusted."

"That can't be right," I tell him. "Not after everything we went through last summer."

He shrugs. "Looks right to me."

We tiptoe around the tree line until we're as close to the porch as we can get without being seen.

Birdie cups her hands and scoops them into a small porcelain bowl before splashing water on her face like she's in some kind of skin-care commercial but in the woods and with way more mosquitos. Her porch railing is lined with all kinds of crystals and candles. Lavender and eucalyptus hang from the roofline.

"Is that Luna's moon water?" I ask.

"I'm pretty sure it's not lemon LaCroix."

Birdie picks the bowl up and pours the rest into her mouth like cereal milk. She swishes and gargles it around before spitting it out like she's the human centerpiece of a very fancy fountain. The water arcs into the air. She sighs before standing and stepping over the candles and crystals to sit in her rocking chair.

"Okay, that was weird," I admit. "But maybe we should just give it a try and talk to her."

"Or maybe she'll know we're suspicious of her and Luna and it'll put a target on our backs," Logan counters.

I cross my arms over my chest and silently *hmph*. There's literally nothing that Birdie could do that would make me feel like I couldn't trust her. Right? I mean, the woman had to defeat her own sister last summer to save the camp. Sacrifices don't get much bigger than that.

As I begin to step forward, she leans back in her rocking chair and kicks her shoes off before propping her feet up on the railing and—

I clap a hand over my mouth to stifle my gasp. "Those are the hairiest feet I've ever seen in my life!"

"Then you haven't seen my Uncle Oscar's feet," Logan mumbles. "But seriously, those toes are straight out of Middle-earth."

Birdie yawns and stretches her arms behind her head, totally unaware that she has an audience.

"Some people are just hairier than others," I say in a desperate attempt to make sense of this.

Logan nods. "Sure. You're actually right about that."

"And it's not just men," I tell him with a finger pointed.

"Never said it was."

I nod. "Cool."

"I'm glad we're on the same page when it comes to body hair," he says.

"Maybe we should just try talking to her during the day after lunch or something. This is sort of weird that we stalked her all the way out to her cabin."

Logan gives me a thumbs-up just as Birdie yanks her leg behind her head like she's some contorting yoga master and it takes my eyes a moment to communicate to my brain what I'm actually seeing. But as Birdie moves her foot repeatedly, it becomes very clear that she's scratching behind her ear.

With her foot.

"Cool. Cool. Cool. Cool. Are you seeing what I'm seeing right now?" Logan asks.

"That depends," I say a little frantically. "Are you seeing Captain B using her foot to scratch behind her ear like a dog?"

"This is too weird," Logan says.

And he's right. We gotta get out of here!

We begin to backpedal as quietly as we can, but of course

I step on the noisiest twig of all time and it snaps so loudly it even startles the bugs.

Birdie sits up straight and alert, her head swiveling from side to side like she's just gotten a whiff of prey.

"Time to run," Logan says.

We take off into the forest as quickly as we can, weaving in and out of trees. Maybe if, for some reason, Birdie can actually smell us, our scent will be so spread out that she'll have a hard time tracking us. But she's not actually . . . part animal or something. There's no way.

My lungs are beginning to burn a little and thankfully Logan shuffles to a stop as we come up on a clearing.

"This is not good," I say in between panting. "Like, this isn't just us jumping to conclusions, right? I know we both wanted to discover something cool this summer, but—"

Logan rests his hands on his thighs as he catches his breath, "Like another ghost! Or a portal to another dimension!"

"A portal would have been so much cooler than finding out my favorite camp counselor is a—"

"Did you hear that?" Logan asks.

Something in the woods rustles and it's getting closer.

Quickly.

I pull my mini flashlight out. There isn't time to run, so here's hoping whoever jumps out of the brush is scared of my flashlight. . . .

CHAPTER TWELVE
Nora

I don't particularly like being outside in the dark, alone, yet that's exactly where I find myself after my heart-to-heart with Luna. I have to make a choice: Do I race down the long but familiar path to my cabin, or do I opt for the shortcut through the woods that Claire showed me and make it to my bunk in record time?

I try the shortcut.

But I quickly realize it's a lot harder to navigate through the woods at night. Just ten (yes, I counted) steps into the brush and my heart is thumping so hard I swear it might leap out of my chest. The final straw is when something fuzzy brushes my bare leg (ew!!!). I chicken out and dart back toward the path as fast as I can.

Nine more steps, eight more steps, seven—

"Ahhh!" I scream, suddenly blinded by a bright, white light.

"Nora?" A familiar voice asks from behind the glare.

I squint. "Maggie?"

"Oh my gosh." She exhales a sigh of relief, lowering her flashlight. "You scared the bejeezus out of us!"

"Why were you running?" Logan asks, looking concerned. "Are you okay?"

"I'm fine. Just spooked. I tried to take a shortcut back to my cabin and got freaked out about getting lost, and then something—"

I don't get to tell them about the gross thing that grazed my leg because there is a sudden, ear-splitting howl.

"What was that?!" I ask, jumping closer to my friends. "Should we run?"

Maggie looks at Logan. "Do you think it's . . . ?"

"We can't outrun her if it is. Let's just hide!" Logan urges.

Before we can do anything, a wolf—a grizzly, fang-toothed flipping *wolf*—bursts through the underbrush. It's the biggest one I've ever seen.

My breath catches in my throat, and I go still. So do Maggie and Logan.

The beast stalks closer to us, baring its teeth and letting out a low, vicious growl. It sniffs at Maggie, who squeezes her eyes shut, before moving on to Logan. The wolf's expression changes and it nudges its snout against Logan's balled-up fist in a way that reminds me of Maggie's dog, Pickle, if Pickle was terrifying and roughly the size of a small car.

Then he moves onto me. My brain tells me to breathe, play dead, hide, and run all at once. Instead, I try to stay as still as possible, even though my knees are trembling. As the wolf gets closer, I can feel the heat of its breath on my face.

It licks my cheek.

I can't help it. I scream. This wolf is going to eat me, and all I can think is I hope Mami takes good care of my Tamagotchi when I'm gone.

I close my eyes and brace for impact, but it never comes. When I open one eyelid to peek at the wolf, I see that it has turned away from me. One of its ears twitches, as if it's listening intently at something in the woods. All at once, the wolf bolts, disappearing into the night as quickly as it arrived.

"Oh my gosh!" Maggie cries, once we're certain the wolf is gone. "We're alive!"

"Are we though?" Logan grips his chest as if making sure he's still all there. "Because I feel like I died for a second!"

"It licked me," I groan. "Like I was a delicious snack!"

"Why did it suddenly run off?" Maggie wonders.

"I think it heard something," Logan says. "But I don't think we should stick around to find out what that something was. Let's go!"

"Freeze!" a voice commands, and we do. It's Luna, wielding a lavender-colored flashlight, and she does not look happy. Her face is twisted in a scowl and her normally light, breezy voice has gone cold. "What exactly do you think you're doing out here?"

"We got lost!" Logan blurts. "And a wolf almost attacked us!"

Luna frowns deeply. "That's why you shouldn't be in the woods after sunset." Her eyes fall on me. "And you, Nora? I'm surprised. Did you take nothing from our conversation?"

My hands go clammy. Great. I've disappointed Luna. "I was just trying to get back to my bunk, and I—"

Luna tsks loudly and puts her hand up. "Never mind. The point is that you shouldn't be out here."

"Mom?" Luna aims her flashlight toward the sound. It's Claire.

"What do you think you're doing, young lady?" Luna demands.

Claire tucks a stray piece of hair behind her ear, not at all fazed. "I came looking for Nora. She didn't come to our cabin after dinner and I wanted to make sure she was okay."

"I'm okay," I say meekly.

Claire turns to her mom. "Why do they look so scared? Did you freak out at them?"

"I did no such thing!" Luna exclaims.

"All good over here?" Captain B emerges from the darkness.

What is going on tonight, and why is everyone suddenly in the middle of the woods?

Luna's face softens at the sight of Captain B. "Yes, yes, of course, Birdie. I heard loud noises and came to check, only to discover some of our campers have gone rogue."

Captain B shakes her head. "It's dangerous out here!"

"And you know the rules," Luna reminds us. "No camper should be wandering around the woods, unsupervised, at nightfall. You could've been hurt, or worse." In a softer voice, she adds, "You scared me."

"And me!" Captain B forks a thumb behind her. "I heard the screaming from all the way out in my cabin."

Luna shakes her head. "Sadly, you are all going to have to be punished for this. I expect all four of you to report to my office first thing in the morning. Understood?"

"Understood," Maggie and I say in unison.

"Yes," Logan says.

Claire rolls her eyes. "Seriously?"

Luna ignores her daughter and turns to Captain B. "Birdie, can you please escort our campers to the main lawn so they may safely head to their bunks? I'm so upset I need to go lie down."

"Of course, of course. You go rest." As Luna saunters away, Captain B turns to us. "What happened tonight?"

"It's my fault," I rush to say. "I needed some fresh air after dinner, so I bailed on these guys. It got dark so fast, though, and I tried to take a shortcut back to my cabin, but I got lost. They came looking for me. I'm really sorry, Captain B."

Captain B scratches her chin, as if considering whether she believes me. "Well . . . all right, then. Let's get you back where you belong." We follow her through the woods, not daring to so much as breathe too loudly let alone talk. When we make it back to the main lawn, Captain B turns to us and puts her hands on her hips. "I can trust you all to go straight to your cabins, right?"

"Right," we murmur.

"I mean it! No funny business. And if you can do that without incident, I'll try to talk to Luna about your punishment," she offers. "Okay?"

"Fine." Claire sighs.

"Thanks, Captain B," Maggie says.

"You bet, Maggie Bananas. Now, good night, you four." Captain B looks off in the distance and sniffs the air a few times. "Is someone roasting hot dogs?" And she wanders off.

"Don't worry about my mom. She'll cool down by morning," Claire assures us. "But why were you guys really in the woods?"

Maggie and Logan exchange a glance.

"We were looking for Nora too," Logan says with a shrug.

Maggie nods, but I can tell she's lying.

Claire has a good point though: Why *were* they in the woods? Were they creeping around trying to conjure ghosts? Or hunt for goblins? Or discover remnants of last summer's vampires? I know whatever they were doing was probably related to something supernatural. I suddenly feel annoyed.

"You were looking for something spooky, weren't you?" When neither Maggie nor Logan answer right away, I cross my arms. "I know you two weren't out there looking for me.

As if you care why I disappeared."

Maggie blinks at me. "What? Don't say that. Of course, we care!"

"But you were really in the woods trying to track down trolls or something," I say. "Admit it."

Logan puts up his hands. "Hey, now. We were absolutely not trying to track down trolls. I don't even believe in trolls!"

"We were at Captain B's cabin," Maggie explains. "We were . . . well, we were spying on her to try and figure out what really happened with Jesse and the wolf attack."

"I knew it!"

"Spying?" Claire shakes her head. "A little much, don't you think?"

Maggie chooses to ignore her. "When we were at Captain B's, we noticed something really weird. She was gobbling up moon water and"—Maggie looks around to make sure the coast is clear before hissing—"out of nowhere she started scratching her ear with her foot like a dog!"

"And her *feet*!" Logan makes a face. "They looked like hairy hobbit feet!" Quickly, he glances at Maggie and adds, "Not that there's anything wrong with body hair, of course."

Claire looks confused. "Huh?"

Maggie presses. "I know it sounds fake, but we're serious! It was like Captain B was turning into some kind of animal. Something really weird is going on!"

Now I roll my eyes. "I'm so sick of hearing how everything that happens at this camp is some kind of conspiracy,"

I say, exasperated. "First you bring ghost-hunting equipment, then you think a creature attacked that cabin, now you're saying Captain B is morphing into an animal? It seems like you *want* something bad to happen to us this summer, just like last year!"

Tears unexpectedly prick at my eyes, and it feels like all the big emotions of the day crash down on me all at once. I suddenly wish I was back at home, fighting with my brothers over who gets the last empanada Mami made and snuggled up beside my Squishmallows.

Maggie's face falls. "How could you say that?"

"So you didn't come to camp this summer hoping something supernatural would happen?" I ask.

When she doesn't answer right away, I know I'm right. And that stinks. I didn't want to be right about this.

Maggie gives me a defiant look. "Even if I did hope for something supernatural, I didn't mean this. And there *is* something off about what happened to Jesse, and something *is* really going on with Captain B. But fine! If seeing vampires with your own two eyes won't convince you that the supernatural is all around us, I don't know what will. Go off with your new best friend and keep pretending nothing's wrong. See if I care!"

Her words sting worse than that time I got bitten by a jellyfish. Rather than retreat, though, anger burns in my chest.

"You're just jealous!" I accuse, even though *I'm* the one who's been feeling jealous lately.

I wait for Maggie to yell back at me, but she doesn't. She goes quiet instead.

"Pretending this isn't happening won't make it true," Maggie says softly. "Let's go, Logan."

She sulks away, and Logan follows.

Once they're gone, Claire lets out a low whistle. "Welp. That sucked."

"Can we go?" I ask, quickly wiping at a hot tear that's escaped the corner of my eye. "Please?"

"Yeah, of course," Claire says gently. "Come on."

Back in the bunk, my head is swirling from all that happened tonight.

I head to the bathroom to splash some cold water on my face. Then I remember the moon water from earlier.

Luna's voice echoes in my mind: *Use a bit of this tonight and feel better.*

I'd do just about anything right now to feel better.

I pull the vial of moon water from my overalls and splash a whole bunch on my face. I even swish it around in my mouth for good measure.

I don't know how quickly that stuff is supposed to work, but I do sleep peacefully that night despite the mess of emotions swirling in me.

When I wake the next morning, I march straight to the bathroom, wondering if that second part of what Luna said will also be true. Can I actually see my inner beauty shining thanks to the moon water?

Yet in the mirror, I look the same as ever.

And what's with this itchy head? Did running through the woods give me fleas or something? I touch my hair to feel for bugs but instead just find a small twig that had been tangled in my curls. Guess I really did sleep soundly.

I try to shake off the disappointment of the failed moon water by forcing a smile in the mirror. Then I do a double take at my reflection.

Is it just me or do my teeth look suspiciously straight and are those pesky hairs on my upper lip gone?

I almost smash my face into the mirror to get a closer look.

Oh my gosh. My little baby mustache is gone and . . . my teeth are *straight*. My teeth are straight! My. Teeth. Are. Straight!!!

Luna was right. The moon water worked!

CHAPTER THIRTEEN
Maggie

"Does anyone else feel like a dance class is scarier than fighting a vampire?" Kit asks as we walk up the trail to the barn.

Evelyn grimaces. "It can't be worse than the etiquette classes my mom made me take last year at school."

"That's just cruel and unusual punishment," I tell her. "I'm stressed about this Moon Ball thing. Are we supposed to have dates? How am I going to know if someone wants to dance with me?"

"We'll dance with you," Evelyn says. "I bet Logan will too. And Nora!"

Kit turns to me as she swats a bug out of her face. "Hey, what's Nora been up to anyway? I've hardly seen you two together."

"Well, it's not like I've seen much of either of you," I say, feeling immediately defensive and then ridiculous for feeling that way. "And I've seen Nora! You just haven't *seen* me *seeing* Nora."

But the truth is . . .

I haven't spoken to Nora in two days. Two! Whole! Days!

That's the longest we've gone without talking at each other's faces since camp last summer.

Not because I'm mad at her or she's mad at me . . . I think. But because we've just been doing our own things. And because every time I see her she's with Claire and I feel awkward going up to them. Then I feel awkward about feeling awkward. We fought, but it wasn't a real fight, was it?

I'm overthinking this. And now I'm overthinking the whole overthinking thing. It's never been hard to be friends with Nora. Our friendship is the easiest thing in the world, but suddenly my brain is working overtime just trying to imagine the right thing to say at the right time.

And apparently, I'm not the only one to notice the sudden divide between us.

The three of us roll up to the barn and Logan splits off from a group of campers to join us as we search for a pocket of open floor space. With nearly the whole camp here, the place is a little crowded.

"Is it weird that I'm kind of excited about this whole dance workshop thing?" he asks.

"It's gotta be better than primal screaming," I say.

"Ooooh, I did Primal Screaming 101 the other day and found it quite therapeutic," Evelyn says in her most proper British accent. "I think my mother would truly benefit from it."

Kit grins. "My dads too."

I can't help but pout. Is everyone getting the swing of camp this year without me?

"I told Luna I used the scream to break my vow of silence. She was very impressed," Evelyn says. "I'm not sure how I feel about her, but I do quite enjoy being a teacher's pet."

I peer over the bobbing heads to see Nora walk in with Claire, who's laughing hysterically at something so charming and smart, I'm sure, that my bestie's just said. I reach over my head and begin to wave. Our eyes meet for just a second before I lose sight of her. Maybe the best thing is to act like everything is normal between us. I don't want to talk about what happened the other night and I bet she doesn't want to either.

All around us campers are itching and scratching from bug bites. There are lots of peeling sunburns and the whole crowd smells like a mix of body odor and aloe vera from the nurse's office to treat sunburns. To says we're missing all the stuff we packed from home to survive two weeks in the outdoors is an understatement.

"Campers," Luna's voice rings from the stage where we trapped Sylvia last summer in a ring of salt. "Welcome to the Moon Ball dance workshop." She sits, perched on a stool, her wild curls puffed up like a lion's mane and the hem of her white floor-length sundress dark with dust from the walking paths.

"Birdie had hoped to join us today to lead today's session,

but sadly she's come down with a highly allergic case of poison ivy. While I encourage each and every one of you to become one with the landscape, please do keep an eye out for our three-leafed friend, who prefers to be admired and not touched. Let's remember today's word of the day is *curiosity*."

"Poison ivy is my worst nightmare," Kit says under her breath.

Logan leans over and whispers in my ear. "Do you think hobbit feet are a side effect of poison ivy?"

"Not any kind of poison ivy I've ever seen."

"Birdie is with me in spirit," Luna continues. "And I honor the goddess in her as I share this dance demonstration on her behalf."

"Um, that's weird, right?" I ask Logan.

"She kind of reminds me of my cousin, Mallory. She's a yoga instructor who changed her name to Stardust."

I shrug. "Not a bad name if you ask me."

"The music please," Luna says and motions to the bearded counselor whose name has turned out to be Leaf, though I'm not sure if that's a real name. He nods and hits play on a Bluetooth speaker.

Luna sits down on the floor with her back to the crowd. The song begins with a long gong noise.

"I guess we're not learning how to line dance," I say.

But everyone is sort of entranced by Luna and her music, even Logan.

I glance around to find that Nora's made her way to the front of the barn and is watching Luna with wide eyes.

At least she seems to think this is as bizarre as I do.

The gong stops and it's followed by five seconds of the longest silence I've ever sat through before there's an eruption of sound and Luna arcs backward and begins to crab-crawl on the stage like we used to do in elementary school PE.

Without warning, she leaps to her feet and moves around the stage like something is yanking her around with invisible strings.

All around me, no one can look away. There are quite a few confused faces, but Luna has everyone's attention, that's for sure.

The music stops abruptly and she collapses to the stage in a human sundress puddle.

"What *was* that?" I whisper.

Luna stands and takes a bow before a slow clap gains momentum. Completely confused by what I've just seen, I join the applause.

No wonder Birdie isn't here. If that's what I was supposed to do in front of a barn full of people, I'd call in sick too.

"And that's what we call modern dance," Luna says. "This type of movement flows through you and forces your body to connect with your surroundings. It requires you to live in the moment. And above all, there are no rules. You can dance on your own. With a partner or a group. You can lie on the ground or spin in circles. This is a chance for your body to interpret your emotions. Now it's your turn. Kick off your shoes. Close your eyes. Open them wide. Whatever suits you."

Kit rolls her shoulders back and begins to stretch. "I always try everything once."

"Famous last words," Evelyn tells her as she sways from side to side. "But it does look sort of fun."

"My school went to the ballet once and there was some modern dance too," Logan says. "This sort of reminds me of that."

The music begins with the sounds of nature and all around me, kids begin to awkwardly sway and shuffle their feet. I really thought we would just be here learning a few ballroom dances or something.

The sound of chirping birds swells and a furious-sounding set of string instruments collide with the chaotic tweets.

A few campers begin to loosen up, including Kit, who lifts her arms in the air and lets her body sway like tall grains of wheat.

Even Logan is really getting into it.

I crane my neck around to check on Nora, who's spinning with her arms spread wide and a huge grin on her face. It reminds me of the times we'd link hands on the playground and spin each other in circles until we were dizzy.

Campers around her step back a bit as she lunges from side to side. Nora took loads of dance classes when we were younger and it always helped when we auditioned for musicals or school plays back home, but I've never seen her let go like this before. She gracefully runs into a leap.

And I'm almost a little bit jealous.

I try to move around a little too. I even close my eyes for a moment to block out everyone around me. But my limbs feel like they're full of cement. This is Primal Screaming 101 all over again!

The music continues and I stop trying, because if I can't be good at it I don't really want to even try.

"Whoa, Nora's got some serious skills," Logan says. "I had no idea."

She leaps again just like she's in *The Nutcracker* or something, but her movements are looser and not so formal.

And we're not the only ones noticing Nora. Other campers have stopped and a circle begins to form around her. Even Luna is paying attention as she proudly beams from the stage with her hands clasped to her chest.

The music finishes and Nora sinks to the ground, flinging her arms out and her head back.

This time when people clap it isn't slow or uncertain like it was for Luna. The applause is thunderous!

Nora's eyes fly open and her cheeks immediately turn pink the second she realizes the whole camp has become her audience. She looks down and covers her face with her hands, like she's embarrassed.

But then Nora grins before she stands and curtsies with a laugh.

That's my best friend! I want to shout. I really didn't know she had it in her. I'm feeling too many things at once to make any sense of it all.

I'm proud of my bestie. I'm sad I never suspected she could let go like that and in front of a crowd of people. But I'm also feeling a little bit like something is wrong with me for not being able to do the same.

If this is anything like what I can expect at the Moon Ball, I might have to take a page out of Birdie's book and roll around in some poison ivy.

CHAPTER FOURTEEN
Nora

It feels like my life has vastly improved since I started using moon water.

Which makes me sound like a weird commercial or something, but I swear it's true.

For one, my teeth are suddenly as picture-perfect as a celebrity's and my face is smooth. At first, I worried it was a fluke but it's been days and both are still looking great, so no braces or waxing for me this fall! I wonder if Mami will let us get a puppy instead. I should ask in my next letter home.

I also feel a lot more like the old, spotlight-loving Nora again. Luna was totally right. I really do need to forget everything except being myself.

All of this has made it so that my and Claire's second visit back to the boathouse with Elijah and the Liams wasn't a huge disaster. In fact, I kind of felt like I belonged. So maybe I *can* be as cool as Claire! Sometimes anyway.

Whether it's the moon water or the crystals or something

else, I'll take it. I even felt okay showing off some serious moves during our dance class today. The way people clapped and cheered for me made me feel as warm and fuzzy as when I perform onstage. I've really missed that rush of confidence. I should've known performing is what would help me feel it again!

"You killed it back there," Claire gushes as we make our way to our next activity. "I had no idea you could dance like that."

My cheeks go pink. "I guess all those dance classes have finally paid off."

"Oh, come on. I've taken a dance class before, but that was more than anything someone could teach. That was *all* you." Then she nudges me with her elbow and drops her voice to a whisper. "And look who's coming our way."

I turn to see Elijah strolling toward us.

"Hey, Nora. Claire." Elijah lifts his chin up in that nod that boys do when they're trying to casually say hello. "Where are you guys heading?"

"Artful Affirmations." Claire makes a face. "Try not to be jealous."

"We're trying to figure out if we'll be making macaroni necklaces or chanting things like, 'I love myself!' or somehow doing both at the same time." I let out a laugh.

Elijah laughs too. "I'm off to Hugging Your Higher Self, whatever that means, so I get it."

"If you were coming to ask us to ditch and head to the

boathouse with you guys, we really can't today. My mom's been on my case about showing up for these classes," Claire says.

"Oh, actually, um . . ." Elijah pauses. "I kind of wanted to ask Nora something?"

A smile spreads across Claire's face. "Well, then, I'll just be over here." And she dramatically steps off to the side, totally not out of earshot, and gives me an over-the-top wink.

Even though Claire is nearby and this is not at all a private moment, I still get nervous all of a sudden. Here is a cute boy! Wanting to talk to me! Alone!

"So . . ." Elijah starts. "Your dance was really good back there. You really went for it."

I laugh a little, trying to hide how jittery I'm feeling. "Oh, um. Thanks! Yeah. I've done a lot of acting at home and I guess I realized I've really missed it."

Elijah nods. "That's cool. I've been missing my basketball friends back home too. I get it."

"Yeah, exactly." I pause. "So . . . what did you want to ask me?" I try to keep my voice as even and cool as possible, even though I am fuh-reaking out inside.

"Well, it's just—you've heard about the Moon Ball, right?" Before I can answer, Elijah rushes to continue. "I mean, of course you have. We were just at dance practice. Obviously. It's just—I know it's probably going to be silly and all, but I was wondering if you wanted to go? Together? With me?"

My stomach does a cartwheel.

Is Elijah really asking me to the dance right now?!

"Oh! Well . . ." I glance over at Claire, who is giving me a celebratory shoulder shimmy. I bite back a nervous laugh that desperately wants to escape. "Sure."

Sure?

Sure?

Of all the ways I could've replied, I choose 'Sure'?!

Thankfully, Elijah doesn't seem to notice, and instead he breaks into a big smile. "Cool," he says.

I practically beam back at him. "Cool."

"I'll let you get to your next class, then. Bye!" He takes off before we can say anything else, and an instant later, Claire is grabbing my hands and we're jumping up and down and I'm definitely squealing.

I have a date to the Moon Ball. And it's a boy I like! I have to tell Maggie! We haven't really talked for a few days, but we've both had a chance to cool down and she's the only person I really want to gush about this with.

"Okay, there's no way I can focus now! Can you cover for me in the Art and Affirmations class?" I ask.

"Always! I'll tell them you just got asked out by a cute boy and you need a moment to process," Claire teases.

"Don't you dare," I warn.

She laughs, heading up the trail. "I would never. Obviously, I'll tell them the raw food lunch gave you diarrhea!"

I roll my eyes at the empty threat (it better be anyway!) and hope I can find Maggie at her next class. It takes some searching before I find her at Sound Bath class, which is thankfully held in the grassy area behind the counselors' quarters. I press myself as close as possible to the side of the building, hoping I'm mostly obscured by the nearby leafy bush.

As part of the class, campers sit in a circle with quartz singing bowls in front of them. Currently, the bowls aren't being used and instead everyone is meditating with their eyes closed. I spot Kit in the circle first before my gaze lands on Maggie. Even though her eyes are shut, too, I wave—just in case she's doing that thing where you pretend your eyes are closed but you're really peeking.

When that doesn't work, I decide to dust off some of the birdcalls Stepdad Steve showed me earlier this summer. I made fun of him for it then, but I'm so desperate to get Maggie's attention, I'll try anything.

I whistle my best impression of a mourning dove, which Stepdad Steve told me sounds like an owl going *who-OOH, ooh, ooh, ohh*. It does nothing to catch anyone's attention, which is probably because we're in the middle of the woods and birds are chirping literally all the time.

On to the next plan.

I grab a small pebble from the ground and try to toss it into Maggie's bowl. The first one misses completely (my strength is musicals, not target practice, okay?), but the second one lands with a loud clang. I take cover again behind the cabin wall just as everyone looks up.

After a beat, I peek around the corner and lock eyes with Maggie. She steals a glance at her counselor—whose eyes are safely shut—and mouths back at me, *What's up?*

From where I'm standing, I put a hand over my heart and hold the other hand in the air, swaying back and forth. Surely this is communicating *dance* to her, right?

But when Maggie's brows furrow in confusion, I give up on trying to communicate with her via charades and army crawl through the grass toward the circle. I nudge Maggie with my shoulder and take a place in the circle between her and Kit, crossing my legs and pretending like I belong.

"Hey guys," I whisper. I lean toward Maggie. "Elijah asked me to the dance."

"What?" Maggie whispers back.

"Quiet, please," the counselor hums from across the circle.

I wait for the counselor to strike the bowl before I speak again.

"The Moon Ball," I say, keeping my voice low. "Elijah asked me to be his date!"

Maggie's eyes snap open at this. "He did?" When I nod, I expect her to tackle me with glee. But instead, she closes her eyes again and simply says, "Nice."

My shoulders slump. "Aren't you excited?"

Maggie waits for another bowl to chime before responding. "Of course I am. I just haven't been thinking about the Moon Ball. I've been really busy with bigger stuff, you know?"

"Right," I whisper back. "Sure."

It hurts to hear Maggie say that, as if my first-ever date to my first-ever dance isn't something big. I almost say as much, but after our argument a few days ago, I think better of it.

Instead, I offer, "I've been thinking about that and all the creepy stuff happening too. Maybe we should take a visit to Howie Wowie and see if he knows what's going on?" I hate all this paranormal stuff, but Howie seems harmless enough.

Maggie casts me a look, and I can't tell if she loves or hates the idea.

"Eyes closed, please," the counselor reminds us. "Final. Warning."

We both oblige.

Then, during the next bowl chime, Maggie finally says, "Okay. Let's do it."

It's a small victory, but I'll take it. Without another word, I scootch away from the circle until I'm behind the cabin wall and out of view.

But I need things with Maggie to get back to normal. And soon.

Apparently, there are some things even moon water can't fix.

CHAPTER FIFTEEN
Maggie

"I've got the BFF blues," I admit as I walk into the cafeteria with Kit and Evelyn. I'd been bummed all morning and the only thing I was in the mood for was moping.

Kit throws her arm around my shoulders. "Will it cheer you up if I skip the zucchini lasagna tonight? I didn't realize how gassy it made me until my own fart woke me up in the middle of the night."

Evelyn takes a tray and then passes one to me and one to Kit. "That was rather toxic," she says.

"Maybe you just need to have some fun and blow off some steam," Kit says. "How about we chow down real fast, skip the after-dinner bonfire, and sneak out to the blob?"

Evelyn holds a hand to her chest with a mock gasp. "Kit, are you suggesting we break the rules?"

"That does sound pretty great," I say as I scoop some broccoli salad onto my plate.

Kit follows behind me. "It's less rule breaking and more

supporting a friend in her time of need with all the fun things we missed out on last summer because of the whole fighting off a vampire thing."

"I fully support this," I tell her.

After scarfing down our food, we slip out of the cafeteria and down to our bunk to change into our swimsuits.

Last summer I would have been way too freaked out to go to the lake at night with all the rumors about Howie pulling swimmers under, but I feel pretty confident saying that Howie is just misunderstood on account of being a ghost. Plus, I haven't been able to check out the blob since it was repaired this year.

The swimsuit I bought this summer is blue boy shorts with white stripes on the side and a matching crop top. Nora and I had gone shopping together with plans to buy matching suits for camp, but everything she wanted had ruffles or sequins and I really liked how sleek this suit made me feel. At the time, Nora was a little bummed, but I didn't think much of it. Now I'm starting to feel like that was just one of the first signs that things between us were changing.

As we approach the blob, the sun is starting to set and we each grab a life jacket. (Kit insists.)

"Sad girl goes first," Evelyn says.

"I guess that would be me." I mount the ladder to the top of the platform, and excitement and nerves begin to sprout in my stomach.

Or maybe that's just the zucchini lasagna.

I look down at the giant blue floating inflatable. It looks like a huge pillow and suddenly it's very far away.

Am I scared of heights? Is this something I never knew about myself?

My stomach gurgles.

"You got this, Maggie!" Kit calls as she climbs up behind me.

I shake my head and do the same trick my mom uses with needles on patients at the hospital. She counts to three, but stabs on two. I used to think it was mean, but really she's just helping people get the scary part over with. Anticipation is the worst. So if I can just jump . . .

"One, two—" And then I jump, fully letting go, my legs flying in the air before I land on the soft, airy blob. It's like a trampoline, but better.

"Okay, now you crawl to the edge of the blob," Kit tells me. "This is the really fun part."

I do as she says. I've seen videos of this part. The kid behind you jumps on the blob and sends you flying. The first time I saw it happen, all I could think was what if a super skinny kid jumps after me and I don't go anywhere? Or worse: What if I jumped after a super skinny kid and sent them flying into a tree or something?

But seeing as the three of us all met when Camp Sylvania was still a weight loss camp last year, I think I'm good. Not that I don't like having skinny friends, but there's something nice about having Kit, Evelyn, and Nora too (even though everything is weird with us right now). It's like they just get me in a way that other people don't.

"Okay, I'm ready!" I call up to Kit as I position myself at the edge. "Do your worst!"

She laughs and without even counting down, takes a running leap off the platform and comes crashing down on the blob.

Without any bit of control over how or when, I go flying up in the air higher than I've ever been without being on an airplane. And it's absolutely thrilling.

I cover my mouth with my hands to stifle my scream. My legs are flailing and it feels like I'm moving in slow motion until suddenly, I'm headed straight down for the water and crashing below the surface. I accidentally gulp down some lake water, but it doesn't matter because my whole body feels like fireworks.

In fact, I hit the water so hard that it takes my life jacket a second to bring me back up to the surface.

"Maggie!" I hear Evelyn call from under the water.

After a few seconds, my head breaks the surface and I feel like I'm glowing with ecstatic energy. I hold a hand to my chest and can feel my heart pounding.

Kit and Evelyn look at me, shocked and a little worried.

I hiccup with laughter.

"Are you okay?" Kit asks.

"That was the coolest thing I've ever done," I tell them as I tread water. "When can I go again?"

"After me," Evelyn says. "But if I don't jump right this minute, I'm going to chicken out."

Kit and I cheer her on as I swim back to the dock and then go again.

We all take multiple turns until we're out of breath and practically passed out on the blob, just lying there under the starry sky and the crescent moon.

"Did that make you feel any better?" Kit asks.

I sigh and let my arms and legs splay out like a starfish. "It definitely got my mind off things for a little while."

"What's happening with you and Nora anyway?" Evelyn asks. "You two go together like the Queen of England—God rest her soul—and corgis."

"That's a good thing, right?" I ask.

"Oh, yes," Evelyn confirms.

I don't want to talk about this. Talking about it makes it real, but maybe it will help too. "It feels like we're different people or something," I tell them. "I thought this would be the summer that we'd always dreamed of. But instead Nora is off with Claire and suddenly she cares about boys and looking cool. Like, she already has a date to the Moon Ball. I didn't even know dates were a thing we were doing!"

"Uh, it's definitely not a thing that all of us are doing," Kit says. "No, thank you."

"I get why that feels weird," Evelyn tells me. "But my mom had me going to etiquette classes since I was little and part of that was learning how to dance with boys and sometimes going to dances with them."

"Really?" I ask. "So you've been on a date before?"

Evelyn rolls over on her side to face me. "Not exactly, but what I'm trying to say is that it doesn't have to be a big deal. Or rather, it doesn't have to matter that Nora wants to go on a date and you're not interested in doing that."

I close my eyes, because I feel absolutely ridiculous saying what I'm about to fess up to. "It's not that I'm not interested."

"Say more," Kit demands.

"It just freaks me out," I explain. "Like everything is happening too fast. Last summer, we still played with dolls sometimes and suddenly crushes and liking people are a thing that we're doing."

"Not all of us," Kit reminds me. "And not because it freaks me out. I just feel like I'd rather hang out with friends. And sometimes I still do play with dolls."

"And that's okay too," Evelyn says. "So . . . Maggie, is there someone you might like? Someone whose name rhymes with schmogan?"

"That's not even a word," I tell her with a laugh. "But I guess if I had to go to the dance with someone and it was more than friends . . . I would probably ask Logan." I duck my head into my life vest like a turtle even though they can't even see me that well in the dark. "Is that so weird?"

"I think the weird part is that it took you so long to admit that to us," Kit says. "So are you going to ask him to the dance?"

138

"I don't know," I say. "But maybe it wouldn't be the weird-est thing in the world . . . I just don't want to seem like all googly eyes all of a sudden about dating and crushes."

"It would be okay if you were," Kit says.

"Totally," Evelyn agrees.

"When did we all get so wise?" I ask.

Kit sits up with her legs crossed and looks up into the sky. "I don't know, but it's definitely not genetic. You should meet my brothers."

That gets a laugh out of me and Evelyn.

The three of us stay there until way past curfew as cabin lights start turning off one by one. Eventually, we climb back onto the dock and sneak back to our cabin, where we lay our crystals out for the night along with our wet swimsuits to dry.

For the first time—basically ever—this place feels like a real summer camp.

CHAPTER SIXTEEN
Nora

There are plenty of things I thought I might do tonight: create makeshift s'mores from Luna's stash of raw ingredients; write a letter home to Mami to tell her about my new, super-straight teeth; daydream about dancing with Elijah at the Moon Ball.

But I absolutely did not expect to get an invitation to have dinner at Luna's cabin.

So imagine my surprise when I get back from crashing Maggie's Sound Bath class and that's exactly what Claire says.

"I'm sorry, what?" I ask.

She starts pacing. "Ugh, I know! The nerve of that woman, invading our dinner as if she doesn't take up all of our days with random nonsense. Dinner is supposed to be our time to relax! Now we have to be stuck with her during that time too?" Claire plops on her bed dramatically. "What. A. Waste."

I let her complain while my mind races. A dinner invitation for me? From Luna? To go to her cabin? A little thrill shoots through me. I know this isn't anything out of the ordinary for Claire, but it makes me feel special to be included. I imagine it's not every day a camper gets this type of invitation. I only hope I make a good impression.

I change out of my day clothes (a vintage Destiny's Child T-shirt knotted over my favorite pair of jean shorts and some Converse sneakers) and into something a little nicer: a romper with adorable lemons printed all over, plus some sandals. Then I free my curls from my braid.

When I emerge from the bathroom, I see that Claire has changed too. She's wearing heavy (contraband!) makeup, a T-shirt with two raccoons driving a car on it and the words LIVE FAST EAT TRASH, and jeans with holes so big Mami would argue they might as well be shorts. Personally, I think the outfit is cute, but I'm not sure Luna will feel the same way. Which is probably the point.

"Ready?" Claire asks.

"Lead the way."

Claire doesn't bother knocking on the door when we arrive, and instead barges right in.

Inside, Luna's cabin is every boho girl's dream. It's decorated with hanging plants, potted herbs, incense and various incense holders, and books with titles like *Discovering Your Inner Goddess* and *Crystal Clear: On Meaningfully Using*

Crystals to Guide Your Spiritual Journey. A moon-shaped suncatcher glints in the window, catching the last of the day's sunlight and making rainbow reflections dance across the cabin.

Light-colored rugs are strewn across the floor, while crystals of all sizes line the windowsills and various shelves. Where there should be a dining room set is a low, round tabletop and a bunch of pillows. Luna's even playing records on a record player.

I notice some family photos but don't get a chance to look closely before we hear Luna's voice.

"Welcome, welcome!" she calls to us from the kitchen. "I'm finishing up dinner. Please make yourself comfortable."

"Impossible," Claire mutters under her breath, kicking one of the pillows that I think was supposed to serve as a place to sit.

"Claire, I've been having some trouble with my laptop. Can you take a look?"

Claire rolls her eyes. "Guess laptops aren't too damaging for *her.*"

"And, Nora, dear? While Claire's doing that, would you mind helping me in the kitchen?"

I look at Claire, who has already opened Luna's laptop and made herself comfortable on a pile of pillows, and shrug.

In the kitchen, the dishes on Luna's countertops hold an explosion of colorful fruits and vegetables.

"Can you help me by chopping up these tomatoes for the

avocado panzanella?" she asks. "I got so distracted with our vegan lemon cheesecake dessert that I got a late start on dinner. Thankfully, the recipe only takes about twenty minutes to prepare—quicker with your help if you're willing."

"Of course. I help my mom in the kitchen all the time," I explain, pleased to be asked.

"Oh, wonderful!" Luna reaches for a moon-print apron and hands it to me. "To keep your pretty outfit nice and clean."

I take the apron and tie it around my waist, hoping it fits. Sometimes thin people—even with the best intentions—forget when you have a bigger body that not everything will fit. I'm relieved when it does. "Thank you." I reach for a knife and start to slice the cherry tomatoes in halves, the way Luna had started doing.

"So, Nora. Tell me more about yourself. Where are you from? What's your family like? What color is your aura?"

Auras? I can't tell whether she's being serious or joking right now. "Oh, um. I don't really know the color of my aura. . . ."

"Oh, what a shame!" Luna thinly slices some red onion. "Mine's indigo, meaning I'm naturally curious, spiritually connected, and gentle."

"That sounds about right." I smile. Even though aura colors aren't my thing, I can tell Luna really believes in it, and it feels nice that she's sharing that with me.

Luna adds garlic, capers, and sliced avocado to a bowl with

the onions. Then she peers at me. "I'm actually quite good at reading people's auras once I get to know them a bit more."

I take this as my cue to answer her other questions.

"Well, I'm from Arlington, Texas, and I live there with my mom and my two other brothers, Junior and Sebbie—Sebastian, really, but I call him Sebbie. My mom and my dad are divorced. He moved a few towns over, so we don't really see him as much, but we do FaceTime with him a lot." I fall into a rhythm chopping the tomatoes as I talk. "And, actually, my mom just remarried."

"What's that been like?" Luna asks, scooping my chopped tomatoes into her bowl.

Hard. Weird. Confusing. These are the first three words that come to mind when I try to explain the recent tornado of changes to my life. Stepdad Steve is nice and all, but I had gotten used to having my mom to just me and my brothers. I miss her.

Then there's Darren, my new stepbrother, who is older than Sebbie but younger than Junior. Darren can be a know-it-all sometimes, always chiming in on conversations he wasn't part of with "um, actually" or trying to boss me around, which is extra annoying because I already have two brothers who do that. The worst part is, instead of being a family of four, now we're a family of six. It makes everything so much harder. Six people to cram into one bathroom, six people to squeeze into one car, six people who all want different things to eat. Sometimes it's so loud in the Whaley-Anderson house now I can hardly hear myself think. I often escape to Maggie's just so I can exist without someone breathing down my neck.

But grown-ups don't usually like to hear that kind of stuff. They say things like, "It'll be fine!" or "Change is good!" or some other unhelpful phrase.

So I choose my words carefully, watching as Luna breaks ciabatta bread into small chunks and tops them with olive oil, garlic, and vinegar. "It's been interesting. . . ."

"I bet," Luna muses. "Parents sometimes don't realize how significant changes like that can be for everyone."

"That's exactly it. There have been so many changes I feel like I've lost count." I shake my head. "Little stuff too. Like, when it was just Mami and me and my brothers, every Sunday, we'd drive to the nearby bakery, and we'd get a loaf of pan de agua fresh from the oven. We'd split it right there in the bakery and add butter and jam and it was the most delicious thing ever. But now the loaf isn't big enough for everyone, so we have to get two, or add other pastries to the order, which doesn't seem like a big deal, but . . ."

"It's still different. And that's hard," Luna finishes.

"Yeah. It's hard," I echo. Even though we're talking about something sort of sad, I realize it actually feels good to say this stuff out loud.

Luna wipes her hands on her apron and leans against the counter. "You know, when I was about your age, my mom and dad surprised me with news that they were having another baby girl. I was livid! At the time, I was perfectly content being an only child and did not want a little sister. It felt like nobody cared what I thought or how I felt, even though my life was changing too. I look back now and can't imagine my life without my little sister. But back then, it wasn't easy." She gives me a sympathetic look. "Hang in there. And know you can always come by and chat if you need to."

I smile at her. "That's really nice. Thank you."

She pats me on the arm. "Of course. Now, if I had to guess . . ." Luna squints at me. "I'd say you strike me as an orange. People with orange auras tend to be thoughtful, considerate, and creative."

"Really?" I ask. That assessment feels like a big compliment, like Luna can see who I really am, deep down.

Luna nods. "I can see it clear as day." She sighs. "Your age though . . . those were some of the toughest years of my life. So much change. And puberty . . . well, that was just cruel." Then she adds a few green leaves to the top of the dish—basil, maybe?—and dusts her fingers on her apron. "This is all set. Can you bring it to the table? I'll be right behind you."

I carefully take the tray of food we've made and bring it into the living area where Claire is scrolling on Luna's laptop. I set it in the center of the table. Since Claire is busy, I wander over to the shelf so I can take a look at some of the photos I noticed earlier.

"You'll never believe it, but Beyoncé dropped a new surprise album yesterday!" Claire exclaims.

I gasp. "What?!"

"Yep. And we're missing it! All because we can't have phones!" She groans.

"I can't believe I'm existing in a world where there's Beyoncé music I haven't heard yet." I frown, going back to looking at the photos.

"Tell me about it," Claire says with a huff.

Up close, I see that there is no shortage of photos of Luna and Claire together, despite none hanging on Claire's walls. Here, at least, they look happy together.

"Isn't it funny how my mom pretends our relationship is so perfect by hanging a bunch of photos of us?" Claire scoffs. "Nobody would know how much we fight just by looking."

"That sounds really hard," I say, meaning it.

"I'm used to it." Claire shrugs, as if it doesn't matter. I know it must though.

Claire goes back to clicking on the laptop and I reach for a photo album that's sitting out, open-faced, almost as if it's been looked at recently. The photos show Luna throughout the years. I pause when I get to a picture of Luna—around my and Claire's age. She wears a cheerleading uniform and her skin is a little red with bumps and scars. She wears thick glasses that weigh heavy on her nose. Her hair is frizzy and wild like it can't decide if it wants to be curly or straight.

It's then that Luna sweeps into the room with a teapot and three porcelain cups, which she places on the table.

"Is this you?" I ask, holding up the album in my hands. "You were so young."

"Oh! I thought I'd cleaned up." Luna lets out a tight laugh. "How embarrassing. No one needs to see those old pictures."

"Oh, I'm sorry. I'll put it back," I offer.

She waves her hand dismissively. "That's all right." Luna comes to stand with me at the shelf, gently taking the photo album into her hands. She runs her fingers over the picture I'd been looking at. "These are painful for me to see, but I take them out from time to time to remind myself of how far I've come. And why I started this camp."

"Painful?" I ask softly. "How come?"

Luna makes a face. "Don't you see those acne scars? That frizzy hair? Those wretched teeth? I was mocked relentlessly for the way I looked. I can still hear some of my classmates." She pitches her voice higher. "'Who told you you were pretty enough to be a cheerleader?' It was awful."

"Sounds like it. I'm so sorry that happened to you." And I mean it. Between Luna having terrible childhood allergies and being bullied by her classmates, I feel sorry for her. I shake my head. "They had no right to say those things."

"No, but they were right, weren't they?"

"Oh, come on, Mom," Claire cuts in. "Don't say that."

Luna lets out a sharp laugh. "But it's true! I mean, just look at her."

I take another look at the photo of young Luna. "All I see is a girl who looks like she could've been my friend."

"Well, that's very kind of you, but unfortunately not

everyone sees it that way. Those classmates made my life torture. I hope no one ever experiences that again. It's why I've been so insistent that Claire try her best to fit in. I don't want her to get hurt the same way I have."

I look over at Claire, whose face has turned to stone. She crosses her arms. "I don't need to be told to fit in. I need you to tell me I'm fine the way I am."

"But the world won't think that," Luna says, shaking her head sadly. "The world is unkind!"

"Then the world is wrong," Claire argues. "Maybe if your parents had told you you were fine the way you were, you wouldn't feel the need for all of this." She motions at Luna from head to toe.

Luna stiffens, snapping the photo album shut. "All right. Apologies for the wait on dinner."

"It's whatever. I fixed your laptop. You're welcome." Claire hands her mom the computer.

"Thank you." Luna places her laptop on a side table. "Now, if you'll both join me over here, we can get started."

Luna motions to a pedestal that holds a ceramic bowl decorated with wolf imagery.

"Before we eat, I'd like us all to cleanse ourselves by dipping our fingers into the water in this special finger bowl. It's from Tibet and is one of my most treasured possessions. The bowl was gifted to me when I visited the Himalayas on a year-long retreat when Claire was in kindergarten."

Claire leans close to me and whispers, loud enough for

Luna to hear, "She missed my kindergarten graduation for that."

"Claire," Luna warns. The tension in the room grows. "Once we cleanse our fingers, we can sit at the table and feast."

I follow Luna's instructions, and Claire does, too, though with less enthusiasm. Then the three of us settle at the table on the floor.

"Where are the utensils?" Claire asks.

"Tonight, we'll be eating with our hands. I've come across this enlightening article on how the metal in utensils can interfere with food's curative properties," Luna explains. "We wouldn't want that, especially because we'll also be drinking this delicious, moon water–infused tea I've just brewed."

"And here I thought we could have a nice, normal dinner." Claire gives her mom a tight-lipped smile. To me, Claire mutters, "It's like she's never heard of Coke."

Using our hands, we serve ourselves some food, while Luna pours tea into each of our cups.

"You'll have to tell me what you girls think of this tea. I'm experimenting with the best ways to ingest moon water. Claire already knows this, but I've been working on my moon-water formulation for years, perfecting its healing qualities," Luna says. "Things really took off when I discovered the Camp Sylvania lake water. It feels like the missing piece!"

"Oh, yes, the moon water is nearly perfect! Except for the mysterious side effects," Claire says in mock enthusiasm. "That you won't give me details on."

"Admittedly, there have been some surprising side effects, but they're harmless. I'm certain I've worked out the kinks now."

My stomach drops hearing this. Side effects? Like what? I've been using a ton of moon water because Claire said it was mostly made of vitamins. Am I going to grow a tail or something?

Claire narrows her eyes at Luna. "Don't you think it's a little risky to be letting a bunch of kids drink moon water because of its supposed healing properties without telling them about the side effects?"

"In this case, the good far outweighs the bad, and if I can help campers with the moon water, I see nothing to worry about." Luna tilts her head toward Claire. "Right?"

"Nothing to worry about, like that time you told me my bunny would be safe while I stayed at Nana's for the weekend and then you gave it away?"

They stare at each other.

"Mr. Whiskers found a good home that weekend," Luna says through gritted teeth. She forcefully rips a piece of ciabatta, and I gulp.

Claire gives Luna the same quiet, calm smile she had when Luna broke all of Claire's makeup. It's eerie and makes me wish there was a way I could army crawl right out of this cabin the same way I did earlier at Maggie's Sound Bath class.

The rest of dinner continues with the two of them going back and forth. My head swivels so much it's like I'm watching an intense tennis match. Claire suggests we skip dessert, and I eagerly agree. Anything to get out of here sooner.

When we're done with our meal, I silently help Luna clear the table and bring the dirty dishes into the kitchen.

"Thank you for dinner," I say, because I know if I don't thank her for the meal Mami's voice will haunt me for the rest of the night.

"Of course. You're welcome here anytime," Luna assures me. "I'm sorry you had to witness all of . . ." She motions to the living-slash-dining room. "That."

A perfectly timed crashing sound comes from the other room.

Luna and I rush into the living area to find the pedestal that had been holding the Tibetan finger bowl has fallen over—and the bowl is now in pieces on the floor.

"Claire!" Luna hisses.

"Whoops! I don't know what happened." Claire holds her hands up and shrugs. "I guess I just wasn't watching where I was going."

Luna starts to pick up the pieces, cradling them in her hands as if they were precious jewels. "It's all right . . . I'm sure it was only an accident."

Yet from the faint smirk on Claire's face, I have a sinking suspicion it wasn't an accident at all.

CHAPTER SEVENTEEN
Maggie

"No one tells you that sound baths make you so hungry," Logan says as I approach his cabin where he sits on the step, waiting for me. "All I could hear there at the end was my stomach growling."

"Well, lucky for you it's build your own burrito night." I'd asked Logan to walk with me to dinner so I could share Nora's stellar idea to contact the camp ghost, Howie Wowie.

Last summer, Howie had warned us about Sylvia's plan by communicating to us in his old, abandoned cabin, so maybe he knows what's really going on here again this summer. No one knows this place like Howie.

I point to a spot on his chin. "You've got something white there under your lip."

Logan blushes. "Uh, that would be my acne cream. I hid it from Luna and Birdie."

"No way!" I exclaim. "I hid mine from them too."

He grins. "Couldn't live without it."

"Ditto." Knowing Logan also uses zit cream makes me feel a little less embarrassed about needing it myself. I guess we're both in the acne club. "I was thinking maybe after dinner, we could skip the bonfire and head out to Howie's old cabin to try and contact him," I say, floating Nora's idea. "If anyone has eyes on this place at all times, it's Howie."

Logan stands up and we begin to mosey up the path. "That would be a great idea if it weren't for the fact that Luna renovated that cabin and put campers in it."

Well, crud. "There has to be another way to contact him, right?"

"You said you saw him in the woods when you got here," Logan says pensively. "And people see him near the lake all the time, so maybe he's somewhere down there."

"Oh!" I say, something just occurring to me. "The abandoned boathouse! If I were a ghost and had been evicted from my cabin, I'd totally hole up in that boathouse."

"Ooooh, solid idea. Me, you, post-burrito ghost-hunting adventure?"

"It's a date," I blurt, and my skin immediately feels like it's coated in flames.

A date? Why would I even use that word? I can think of a million other words to use besides *date*. Plan! Appointment! Meeting!

But Logan is unfazed. He groans as his stomach growls and we begin to pick up the pace toward the cafeteria.

Who even cares about dates? Or being asked on one? Or

going on one? What even is a date? Can something be a date if you don't have a car or a place to take someone? Like with Elijah and Nora going to the Moon Ball. We're just all going to walk from our cabins up to the barn and awkwardly cling to the walls and avoid eye contact with each other. I actually can't imagine anything more miserable than going on a date!

But if Elijah wanted to go with Nora and Nora wanted to go with Elijah . . . does that mean that Logan wants to go with . . . someone? Someone like me? I haven't been able to stop thinking about the possibility since last night with Kit and Evelyn.

And maybe the thought of going to the Moon Ball isn't so, so awful. Maybe it would be just like going with a friend, and if that's the case, why put a label on it at all? I wonder if I should ask Logan before someone else does or even worse, before he asks someone else.

This whole dating thing is messy. Maybe even messier than the paranormal.

"I can't believe we never discovered this place last summer," Logan says as we step off the lighted path and toward the boathouse at the edge of the property.

"We were pretty busy if you remember," I tell him. "And I bet this place was covered in thorny shrubs last year." I was going to ask Nora to come with us, but she was talking to Elijah and I didn't want to ruin their vibe with a silly ghost hunt.

Logan kicks the door of the boathouse open with the toe of his sneaker and we step inside and right through a cobweb, the both of us making *blech* noises and waving our arms around before I pull the small flashlight out of my pocket, and we find two crates to sit on.

"So how did you get in touch with Howie last time?"

"It was more like he contacted us. He used the leaves on the cabin floor to spell out words."

"Whoa, that's pretty trippy," Logan says. "So we wait?"

I nod. "We wait." What else can we do?

We sit there in silence for a few minutes before Logan makes a really bad attempt at making shadow puppets in front of the flashlight while the thought of the Moon Ball gnaws at me.

"Are . . . are you excited about the Moon Ball?" I ask as he tries to make a shadow bat.

"I haven't really thought much about it. Just really been thinking about Jesse and, I know this is bizarre, but Birdie's feet. That was just so weird."

"Super weird . . ." I can't help but think about the last few days and how I feel these invisible strings holding me back for no reason. Like with the primal scream and the dance workshop. Why can't I just let go? Maybe it's the fear of what other people think or what I'll think of what other people think. But I don't want to be my mom's age and sitting around wondering *what if*? But why can't everything feel like I'm being flown off the blob and into the air?

I guess if I'm going to loosen up, I just have to do it, and what better time to start than now? The transition from Birdie's feet to this next question is supes awkward, but here goes . . . "Uh, Logan, I was actually wondering if you wanted to go to the Moon Ball . . . together?"

He chokes on spit or thin air or something, like I've just startled him, and then goes into a hacking coughing fit.

I jump up. I never learned CPR! I skipped that day of health class to go to a fancy spa for Mom's birthday last year. They had a whole snack bar with M&M's organized by color.

"Are you okay?" I frantically ask.

He continues to cough, but manages to bark out a resounding, "YES!"

I plop back down on my crate. "You scared me for a minute there."

He clears his throat and wipes tears from his watering eyes. "I mean, yes, I am fine. But I was saying yes to the Moon Ball. Of course I want to go with you."

Of course? Of course he wants to go with me? To the—

Before I can even fully process what he's said, something crackles in a dark corner of the boathouse.

"Did you hear that?" I whisper.

The crackling noise happens again in a short quick burst.

Logan nods and swings the flashlight around the dark room, which has only one single sliver of moonlight leaking in from a dirt-caked window on the other side of the building.

The flashlight pauses on a dusty old stereo in the corner.

We both sit there in complete silence, waiting and hoping for—

With a sudden shock of noise, the stereo comes to life, lighting up this time and with the volume turned up all the way as the dial spins back and forth, jumping from top of the charts music to droning talk radio.

"Howie!" I gasp as we both rush to the corner where the stereo sits.

Logan begins hitting a few buttons and one causes a lid on top to open. "No CD inside," he says before grabbing the cord and following it to the outlet . . . except the stereo isn't plugged in.

Whoa.

Logan looks from the unplugged cord to me and then to the radio again, which looks like it is one-hundred-percent possessed.

I turn the volume down a little bit so that we don't attract any unwanted camp staff attention. "I really, really hope this is Howie communicating with us," I say. "And not some demon trying to trick us into releasing him from his stereo prison."

"An old boom box is a pretty genius place for a demon to live," he admits. "But Howie, if you're out there, we're listening, buddy!"

The dial spins to a song that sounds like Mom's favorite Britney Spears song and a nasally singing voice says, "Oops!"

"Oops?" I echo.

The dial spins again to a stuffy newscaster. "The splash caus—"

Logan looks around like Howie might just be hovering above us. "Oops? Splash?"

Again, the station changes to a country western–sounding voice slowly singing, "Troubleeeeee . . ."

"This is, uh, pretty doom and gloom, Howie," I call out to him. "If you can even hear us wherever you are. We are speaking to Howie, right?"

The speakers crackle with static for a moment and Logan gives me an eerie look. We could be talking to anything—or anyone. If I've learned anything in the last year researching the paranormal, it's that the spirit world is not to be messed with.

"Howdy!" an old-timey voice shouts.

"I guess we can take that as a yes?" Logan ventures.

The static starts up again before the stations begin to change at a rapid pace, only catching syllables of songs and voices.

"Hair."

"Oof."

"Hair."

"Oof."

"Hair . . . ," I say.

"Oof," Logan mutters.

"Hair."

"Oof."

"Hair."

"Oof."

I gasp as it hits me. How didn't I see this before? All the clues were right there. Logan and Jesse's destroyed cabin. The howling. Birdie's hairy feet.

Logan and I turn to each other, and I can see it's hit him too. In unison, we both say something that feels impossible and yet totally true.

"Werewolf!"

CHAPTER EIGHTEEN
Nora

The dinner at Luna's helped me better understand just how tense things can be between her and Claire. I thought Luna breaking Claire's makeup that second day of camp was bad, but things are way more intense than I initially thought. It really puts Stepdad Steve's corny thumbs-up habit into perspective.

Since then, I've started to notice little ways Claire is rebelling against her mom. She started leaving contraband items out in the open like she's daring someone to catch her. (Apparently many of the books she'd brought had actually been hollowed out on the inside, and contained precious items like eyeliner, gum, and lipstick. Genius.) She's been skipping morning workshops without telling me where she's going. And she even used a Sharpie to draw a mustache and angry eyebrows over Luna's face on the Camp Sylvania poster outside the main office. I'll admit that one made me laugh out loud.

But Claire hasn't actually said anything out loud about how she's feeling, so I haven't, either. Instead, I'm trying to be as nice as possible. It seems like she needs it. Thankfully, today is the big Water Therapy event, which is supposed to be a day of goofing off and having fun. I think we could all use it. Luna has even promised to set up a slip and slide down by the lake!

I rub the sleep from my eyes and head into the bathroom to brush my teeth.

Only, I nearly scream when I catch my reflection in the mirror.

Peeking out from beneath my armpits are gigantic tufts of hair! And I'm not talking about normal, puberty-induced armpit hair. It looks like I've slapped two unruly wigs under each of my pits! What is going on?! How is it possible I've traded in a hairy upper lip and crooked teeth for Chia pet armpits? This must be one of those "mysterious side effects" Claire mentioned the other night!

Before I can go into full-on panic mode, I'm startled by a noise coming from the other end of the cabin. When I look over, there's Claire, climbing in through the window. I do a double take, glancing between her and the empty bed where she should've been.

I cross my arms, hoping it's enough to conceal my Chewbacca pits. "Claire?"

"Oh!" Claire gasps and her hand flies to her chest, as if *I've* scared *her*, when she was the one sneaking in through our window! "I thought you might still be asleep. I, um, went for an early morning walk."

I raise an eyebrow. "And came back through the window?"

Claire shrugs, walking over to her bed and kicking off her boots. They land with a loud thunk. "I didn't want to wake you. Plus, I'm actually stealthier sneaking in and out of windows than doors. Don't tell Luna." She gives me a devilish grin.

"Ha, yeah. I won't," I say, though I'm not so sure I buy that she was out for a walk. Claire has never been an early riser, especially not before having breakfast.

What could she have been doing? And with who? "What's with the pose?" Claire asks, motioning toward my hands, which I've buried under my arms in an attempt to hide the hair.

Now it's my turn to laugh nervously. "Just warming up my hands!"

She rolls her eyes. "You don't have to lie, Nor. I have some disposable razors you can borrow if you want to shave before Water Therapy today."

And then it hits me: I'm going to need to be in a bathing suit today. With the hairiest armpits in existence! Given how quickly this mop of hair grew—I swear there was *nothing* there last night before bed—I don't even trust it won't grow back while we're splashing around today. I'm not about to take a chance that the whole camp discovers I've morphed into part-Wookiee.

Guess I'll just wear a T-shirt over my swimsuit. Better safe than sorry.

Because life is sometimes cruel, the only clean T-shirt I have is a black pajama top, which will do nothing but soak up the sun's hot rays.

Even worse: it's a *Cats: The Movie* shirt that my brothers bought me for Christmas. I love musicals, but that movie was so cringe it became a running joke in our house. I only packed this shirt because of how cozy it is to sleep in. I never planned for all of camp to see me in it!

All I can do is turn it inside out and hope for the best.

"You look like you're going to a slumber party rather than Water Therapy," Claire teases as she and I head toward the hill where the slip and slide has been set up.

I sigh. "Trust me, the oversized T-shirt and shorts weren't my first choice, but it's all I had."

Though I used one of Claire's disposable razors to shave my armpits, I can practically feel the hairs already starting to grow back. The T-shirt was the right choice—even if it means no one gets to see my adorable glittery bathing suit.

Thankfully, everyone is so pumped about the gigantic slip and slide that they don't pay much attention to me.

I have to admit: it is pretty awesome. Luna has managed to set up the biggest slip and slide I've ever seen, with sprinklers running along either side for maximum splashing. Luna says she's using charged moon water so that all of us can get a "gentle misting" on our way down.

"Hey!" a voice calls cheerily. I see Maggie, in her blue-and-white swimsuit, smiling and waving as she and Logan make their way toward me and Claire.

I smile back. "Hey guys! You excited for today?"

Logan nods. "Definitely. Besides the blob, this is the most normal thing we've gotten to do at camp so far."

"Tell me about it," Claire agrees. "I bet we can get some serious speed on this thing too."

As they start to chat about how fast they think they can go on the slip and slide, Maggie grabs my elbow. "I have something wild to tell you later," she whispers.

My eyes go big. "Don't leave me hanging!"

"I know, I know, but I don't want anyone to overhear. Find me later and I promise I'll spill everything." She squeezes my arm. Then her eyes flicker over my T-shirt, and her brows furrow in concern. "You okay?"

I know this is her way of asking if I'm feeling shy about my body today. In an instant, she's picked up on the fact that I'm wearing a T-shirt instead of the bathing suit we'd excitedly picked out together. As fat girls, we've had long talks about our bodies and how others always seem ready to judge—if not with their words, then definitely with their eyes. We made a pact last summer to forget what others think and proudly rock our bathing suits. She must be wondering what changed for me. It's enough to make me want to tackle her in a huge hug.

I put my hand over hers and squeeze back. "I'm good. Promise."

"Let's grab our spots. The line's starting to get long!" Claire says as she begins walking toward the crowd of campers.

I follow her. Maggie and Logan are just behind us, with Kit and Evelyn trailing a little farther back, and we take a place at the end of the line.

While we wait, we watch as campers ahead of us each take their turns on the slide. Sara Park surfs down like she's riding a wave, JJ Richardson makes a Superman pose, April McGrady points her toes like the graceful ballerina she is, Quinn Davis goes down headfirst. Everyone is having a great time.

"Hey, Nora," a familiar voice says from behind me. When I turn, I see it's Elijah, and I sort of wish the ground would eject me out into space. I'd so rather he were seeing me in my cute bathing suit rather than my inside-out *Cats* shirt!

I try to hide my inner panic with a smile. "Hi, Elijah. Have you been down the slide yet?"

He nods, pushing some of his curly hair away from his eyes. "Twice. The Liams and I made sure to get here before the crowd so we could pack in as many turns as possible."

"Good thinking! Any tips?"

"About halfway down, the slide swoops up into a small hill. If you close your eyes during that part, your stomach will do that flippy feeling like when you're in the car and you go down a big hill," he says, grinning. "I love that feeling."

I laugh. "Me too! I always used to tell my parents my stomach felt like it was flying."

"It really does!" Elijah glances toward where Big Liam and Dimples are waiting for him. "I should get back in line. They're waiting for me. I just wanted to say hi."

My insides flutter at that and I bite back a huge smile. "I'm glad you did."

He starts to jog toward his group. "Don't forget to close your eyes!"

"I won't!" I call to him.

Once he's out of earshot, Maggie nudges my arm. "So that's who asked you to the dance? No wonder you were so happy!"

I laugh, nodding.

"They're adorable, right?" Claire smiles at me. "You really are."

"Thanks, Claire."

Then she claps her hands together. "Ooh, we're up next!" When it's officially her turn, Claire jogs back a few paces so she can get a running start.

"Count me down!" she calls to us, stretching her legs.

Together, Maggie, Kit, Evelyn, Logan, and I chant, "Three . . . two . . . one . . . go!"

Claire bolts toward the slide and yells, "Theydies and gentlethems, it's been real!" Then she extends her arms above her head and dives onto the slide on her belly, letting out a loud hoot the whole way down.

My journey down the hill is much less thrilling. I climb onto the slide and sit, using my hands to give myself a good push. Between the water and the hill, I gain some decent speed and have fun going down, even if I do feel a little self-conscious about being the only one in a T-shirt. I make sure to take a moment to close my eyes, though, and Elijah's right! My stomach did feel like it was flying.

Logan's next. Claire and I watch from the bottom of the hill. He chooses to lie down like Claire, but on his back and feet first instead. He scoots down awkwardly at the start, then manages to catch some serious speed and races to the bottom.

"Nice one!" I say, holding out a high five to Logan.

He happily accepts. "Thanks!"

Finally, it's Magpie's turn. When I look up at her, I realize her bathing suit is now covered with a baggy *Les Misérables* T-shirt, and my heart swells. She must've left the line and raced back to her cabin to grab a shirt so I wouldn't feel singled out. Because that's Maggie—kindhearted, loving, thoughtful Maggie. My best friend in the whole wide world. And sure, we fought, but best friends fight sometimes. The thing that makes best friendships so strong is getting over the rough patches.

I cup my hands around my mouth and scream, "Yeah, Maggie!!!"

And she breaks into a big grin before getting a running start and jumping onto the slip and slide, yelling, "Woohoooo!"

Logan and I cheer for Maggie her whole ride down. As she gets off the slide, I throw my arms around her.

"Is that a *Les Mis* shirt?" Claire snorts from behind us. "Musicals are so corny."

I turn to her. What is her deal today? With a scowl, I snap, "Judging what other people like is what's actually corny."

Her whole face reddens. "Sorry," she mutters sheepishly.

"It's okay," Maggie says, and I admire her willingness to let it go, even though Claire was being mean for no reason at all. "As long as I can go first when we take our next turn on the slip and slide."

Claire smiles. "Deal."

CHAPTER NINETEEN
Maggie

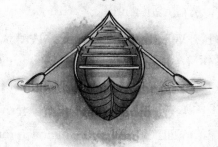

Turns out wearing your T-shirt during slip and slide really slows down your momentum when you're flying downhill on your belly. Or at least it did until my *Les Mis* T-shirt bunched up around my head, completely blinding and suffocating me. For a second there, I thought I was frighteningly close to becoming Howie's eternal bestie. But then my body crashed into a group of campers like a bowling ball hitting a cluster of pins, and I could breathe again.

"That really was pretty epic," Logan says with his towel thrown over his shoulder. He scratches at a cluster of red bumps on his arm. "I think that bug spray Luna gave us attracts bugs more than it repels them."

"I did see a kid scratching his back against the trunk of a tree the other day. He was covered in mosquito bites. And the sunscreen is total junk too." Another reason I didn't mind wearing the T-shirt today was to protect my already pink shoulders from burning even more.

Logan groans. "So what did Kit and Evelyn say when you dropped the big hairy bomb?"

"What big hairy bomb?" Evelyn asks, her chest heaving as she stumbles off the slip and slide with Kit just behind her.

I turn to Logan with my best innocent smile.

"You haven't told them," he confirms.

"Told us what?" Kit asks.

"Uhhhh . . ." I glance over my shoulder and take their hands as I drag them out of earshot of any other campers. Logan jogs behind us.

"So," I say, "I just want you both to know that . . . ummm . . ."

"Spit it out," Evelyn demands as politely as possible.

I look to Logan and he nods, so I do. "Werewolves. We've got werewolves."

"Not again," Kit says with a moan.

Evelyn sighs and starts walking back up to the slip and slide.

"Where are you going?" Logan calls after her.

Evelyn pauses and says over her shoulder, "To take another turn on the slide. Just because we have to save the camp again doesn't mean I'm not going to have fun."

Kit shrugs. "She does have a point."

"So y'all will help?" I ask.

"I guess things were getting a little boring without a paranormal catastrophe if I'm being honest," Evelyn says. "But yeah, I'm gonna take another run on the slide. Let us know how we can help with this wolfy dilemma!"

"Meet us at the boathouse in an hour!" I call.

She gives me two big thumbs-up and keeps on walking.

"That wasn't so bad," Logan says as Kit runs to catch up with Evelyn.

"Yeah, is it weird that our friends are unfazed by a werewolf outbreak?"

"That's a question for another day," Logan says.

As we approach the boathouse, I hear a shriek and immediately dash inside, my flip-flops slapping against the rickety wood floors.

Kit and Evelyn stand huddled together on top of a crate. "Are y'all okay?" I ask, immediately checking to see if the boom box is going haywire again, but it's just as dusty and lifeless as it first appeared to be. "Was it Howie again?"

"Unless he's suddenly in the business of possessing little gray mice that are definitely trying to murder us," Evelyn says with her eyes squinted.

I shiver. "Okay, I *do* hate mice, but Kit, didn't you have a pet mouse named Rudy when you were a kid?"

Logan slides in through the door, panting. "What'd I miss?"

"I did," Kit says as she steps down from the crate and holds a hand up to help Evelyn down. "And yeah, Rudy was my buddy. RIP Rudy. Mice are totally friends, but I kind of got caught up in the moment, I guess."

Evelyn looks around warily before stepping down. "Did we have to meet in a mice-infested boathouse?"

"Singular," Kit reminds her. "Single mouse. He's more scared of you than you are of him—or her."

But Evelyn isn't buying it as she sits down on the crate and pulls her legs up so they're not touching the floor.

"We had to meet here because Howie communicated to us through the boom box." I motion to the giant silver stereo in the corner. "And who knows if moving this behemoth will mean we can't tune in to Howie for whatever reason?"

"Ghosts can be very finicky," Evelyn says as Logan begins to spin the dials on the stereo. "No offense, Howie."

Logan shakes his head. "I'm not getting anything on this."

"Too bad there isn't some kind of ghost hotline we could just call," I mutter to myself as I pace around the room before stumbling upon an old cobweb-covered chalkboard mounted on the wall. It looks like it was used for some kind of scheduling or something and even has a few old camp stickers stuck to the corner.

I use my towel to wipe away the dust and webs before finding one little stubby piece of chalk. "What do we know?" I ask. "Making a list helped last summer, so maybe it can help us again."

"It can't hurt," Evelyn says. "But let's make it quick before that mouse returns with an army of his closest friends."

"Transformation!" Kit offers. "Werewolves transform based on the phases of the moon, right?"

Logan strolls over to me with his chin cradled in his hand. "Do they know they're werewolves though? I've read a few books where people just wake up confused after a night of wolfing out."

"And what about packs?" Evelyn asks. "Don't wolves travel in packs?"

I write down all their points, my penmanship sloppy but still sort of legible. "And what about an alpha? Isn't there always a leader? Would that make Luna their leader?"

Kit's brows furrow. "Luna is bizarre, but I can't imagine her as a wolf. . . ."

"I'm pretty sure they're allergic to silver," Logan says.

I write that down as I wonder aloud, "Do you think they can still transform when it's cloudy outside?"

The door to the boathouse swings open and Evelyn jumps up on the crate again as if the army of mice would just choose to walk right through the front door.

"Whoa, looks like somebody else found our spot," one of the Liams—the one with blond hair—says as he steps in behind Claire. The other Liam, Elijah, and finally Nora spill in.

I frantically search for my towel to wipe away the evidence of our discussion on the chalkboard, but Claire is too quick.

She laughs. "Are you guys seriously talking about werewolves?"

"This is actually a private conversation," I tell her. "But

um, Nora, you can totally stay."

Nora looks from me to my scribbled notes on the chalkboard and then back to me again. She looks confused and a little annoyed, like the time her mom said she didn't get the humor of *Barbie Dreamhouse Adventures*. (Tragic, TBH.)

The other Liam lets out a howl and beats his chest. "I could totally beat a werewolf in a fistfight."

"Calm down there, Captain Meathead," Claire says. "Pack leader?" she reads from the board. "Luna? Are you serious? My mom couldn't be that cool if she tried."

"Uh, I'm pretty sure there's nothing cool about terrorizing a camp full of kids and casually turning people into wolves against their will!" I say with a little bite.

"Let's get out of here," Claire says, "and let this little make-believe club finish their meeting. What's next? Killer mermaids in the lake?"

The Liams and Elijah both laugh, and Nora is suddenly finding the floor to be the most interesting thing in the world.

"That's actually not that far-fetched," Logan says, but his voice trails off as soon as he realizes that this is totally not the right audience.

The guys begin to file out as I say, "Hey, Nora, I really need to talk to you if you want to stick around."

She takes a step toward me, but then Claire grabs her by the wrist. "Actually, Nora was supposed to borrow my razor, right, Nora?"

Nora's cheeks flare a deep shade of pink. "Uh, right. I'll catch up with you later, Maggie."

My shoulders slump as the door shuts behind them.

"I bet they won't be laughing when they end up being bitten by a werewolf," Logan says.

"I really should have asked my parents to get me a rabies shot before this summer," Kit mutters as she examines the chalkboard.

Evelyn shrieks as a mouse skitters across the floor and into a small hole in the floorboards.

I lean against the frame of the windowsill as Nora follows Claire into the trees toward their cabin. "That was weird."

Who even cares about shaving when you're at camp anyway?

CHAPTER TWENTY
Nora

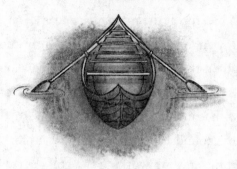

I'm barely listening to Claire at dinner as she drones on and on about how she can't understand why Big Liam hasn't yet asked her to the Moon Ball. I'm actually not sure which of the Big Liams she's even talking about, and at this point, I hardly care. Not when Maggie's been shooting me daggers from across the cafeteria. I guess I deserve it, since I ditched her when she said she really wanted to talk to me.

But I'm kind of annoyed too. Maggie and I were supposed to do some investigating *together*! Instead, she invited Logan, Evelyn, and Kit, and they've decided it's werewolves at Camp Sylvania all on their own. If I hadn't stumbled across them in the boathouse, would Maggie have told me about it? Am I even part of this whole paranormal investigation at all anymore?

And what's up with Claire calling the shots about whether I should hang with Maggie? If I want to be annoyed at Maggie, that's one thing. It's not cool for Claire to decide for me.

Ugh. What a mess.

I make a pit stop at the main office to grab any mail that's arrived. In my cubby is a letter, and I instantly know it's from Mami, based on the bubbly scrawl on the envelope.

She tells me about how Sebbie got banned from the community pool because he kept doing backward flips off the diving board (sounds about right), how Junior already got promoted at his new job working at a golf course (who knew Junior could be good at anything but irritating me?), and how Darren is excelling at math camp (yawn). As for her and Stepdad Steve, they bought a new refrigerator.

Mami writes that she's proud of me for all my new adventures, and most importantly, that she misses me. For some reason that part makes me feel like crying. I thought she might not miss me at all now that she's got Stepdad Steve. I read the letter over and over, hearing her voice in my head. It feels like a warm hug.

I'm still thinking of the letter that night after I finish my bedtime routine, which now includes a healthy splash of moon water plus an armpit shave before bed. Even though I'm tired from the day, I find myself missing home and unable to fall asleep.

Claire must assume I'm knocked out, though, because it isn't long before I hear what sounds like a window sliding open. I keep my breathing steady, as if I really am asleep.

Yet the second I hear the loud thunk of her Doc Martens on the ground below, I bolt upright. I'm going to follow her and figure out why she's been sneaking out.

A secret mission! God, if things between us were a little better, Maggie would eat this up.

Quietly, I stuff a pillow under my blanket so it looks like my sleeping body (I can thank my perpetually rule-breaking older brothers for that trick), shove on some shoes, grab my flashlight, and tiptoe out the front door to follow Claire.

She's quick, but after years of performing onstage, so am I, and I easily keep up with her as she winds down the dark trails of camp and to the cafeteria. Her stride is confident, like she's done this a bunch of times before, and it makes me wonder how often she's been sneaking out while I'm having midnight dreams about my adoring fans giving me a standing ovation for my sold-out Broadway performance (it could happen!).

While Claire slips inside the cafeteria, I rush around to the side of the building to peer in through the windows. Flashlight in hand, she disappears from the dining area into the kitchen, where the staff stores and prepares the food. A few moments later, Claire emerges with an armful of . . . huge, frozen steaks?

Raw meat?

Why would Claire want . . . Wait!

Is Claire the werewolf?!

My mind swarms with a zillion ideas all at once, but I

shake them away knowing I can't get lost in my thoughts right now. *Focus, Nora!*

Claire uses her foot to open the cafeteria door, then strides over to the clearing by the moon-water pool. I duck behind some brush (which I really hope isn't secretly poison ivy or something) and watch. Even though it's almost impossible to see what she's doing in the darkness, I study Claire until she heads back to the cabin.

Once I'm sure she's gone, I creep closer to the moon-water bath. Under the glow of my flashlight, I can now clearly see that the "steaks" are really some kind of compressed tofu called I Can't Believe It's Not Steak! (because Luna, obvs). Other than that, though, nothing seems amiss. Was Claire really sneaking out at night to steal some gross tofu steaks and let them rot by the moon-water pool? What kind of prank even is that?

A rustling sound from the woods snatches my attention. My body freezes. I really don't want to get in trouble for breaking the rules again!

But panic shoots through me when I realize it's not Luna or Captain B or any other camp counselor.

It's a HUGE. FLIPPING. WOLF.

The hulking figure slowly emerges from the woods, sniffing and snarling at the ground. The hairs on my arms stand up, and I go as still as possible.

As it heads toward the "steaks"—the ones I'm standing *right next to*—I realize this is the same wolf from the other night. The one who wanted to eat me as a tasty snack! I worry the same thing will happen again, but the wolf seems far too distracted by the food. As it eats, I start to quietly inch away, but I step on a twig and it snaps, drawing the wolf's eyes right to me.

Without hesitation, I run.

The sound of the wolf's footsteps as he bounds after me sends a chill down my spine.

It's gaining on me!

As I scramble to put distance behind us, I feel sweat start to gather on my neck, and my limbs are trembling so hard I worry I've turned to jelly. Then I trip over the root of a tree.

My whole body crashes to the ground, and so do my hopes of getting out of here alive.

The wolf creeps closer to me, and I let out an involuntary whimper, covering my face with my hands.

It's over, I think, breathing hard. *I bet I'll taste delicious compared to those tofu steaks!*

I jump when something cool and wet touches the back of my hand. Peeking through my fingers, I see the wolf isn't attacking me at all. Instead, it gently nudges me with its snout, the same way it had with Logan's hand the other night.

Slowly, so as not to scare it, I uncover my face to get a better look at the wolf. It's seated obediently, tail wagging, like a dog.

This close, I can see the wolf has one brown eye and one green eye.

I gasp. There's only one person I've ever known to have mismatched eyes!

"Jesse?" I whisper.

The wolf licks my cheek in response.

Holy cow!!! Maggie was *right*.

Worst of all: Claire seems to know all about it. And maybe her mom does too.

CHAPTER TWENTY-ONE
Maggie

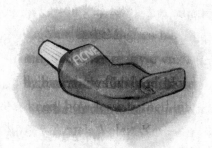

The next morning, I sit on the edge of my bed while Evelyn and Kit are still snoozing and apply my medicated acne cream. After seeing how well this stuff works, I haven't gone a single day without it since Mom first picked it up at the pharmacy. Even Evelyn borrowed some to use on an especially angry nose pimple and then Kit fessed up to hiding her dandruff shampoo during Luna's big sweep for contraband, so I guess Logan and I aren't the only ones cheating on Luna's rules. Though I'll admit, the tea tree shampoo and conditioner Luna's put in all the shower stalls isn't that bad.

Still, nobody—and I mean nobody—is laying a finger on my zit cream.

As I rub in the last of my cream, the cabin door rattles with a knock and I quickly slide the tube inside my pillowcase before hustling over to the door.

"Who is it?" I whisper, trying not to wake my bunkmates.

"Maggie, it's me. Nora!" she whisper-shouts back to me.

I cross my arms over my chest, feeling suddenly prickly. "*Now* you want to talk! Are you sure you don't need to shave or something?"

"Maggie, come on!" Her voice is still quiet but urgent.

I huff, standing my ground and quickly glance over my shoulder to make sure Kit and Evelyn are still asleep.

Nora's not been a very good friend for the last two weeks. She's constantly choosing Claire or boys over me, and she refuses to take me seriously. We've never really fought before, and I hate the queasy feeling growing in my stomach, but I'm done pretending my feelings aren't hurt.

"Maggie," she says again more softly. "I'm sorry. I really am. I should have stuck around yesterday in the boathouse. You said you needed to talk to me and I blew you off."

"It's not just yesterday. It's ever since we got here, Nora. I feel like you're pushing me further and further away."

There's a long silence and I wonder what she's thinking in that super pretty and mostly perfect head of hers. "You're right."

That was totally unexpected. "I am?"

"I didn't mean to. It's just, you have Logan and you guys have all your ghost-busting stuff, and I wanted something of my own. But I *never* wanted to push you away. You're my best friend!"

"You're my best friend too," I say softly.

"And Claire's a jerk!"

I have to laugh at this, because yeah, Claire is kind of a jerk.

"I guess I'm sorry too," I say, leaning up against the door as Kit begins to grumble awake. "I was so focused on looking for something supernatural that I wasn't really seeing *you*."

"Yeah, well, speaking of seeing me," says Nora, "maybe you can open the door now, bestie?"

I feel this big bright space in my chest like all this pressure that's been building all week has just lifted off. I'm so glad to have my BFF back. I pull open the door ready to give Nora the biggest hug of all time . . . but instead I scream. Like a nearly primal scream!

Because standing on the other side of the door is a wolf.

Or no, it's Nora, but she's grown a wolf's *nose*.

"Yeah," says Nora, her whiskers twitching. "That's the other thing I needed to tell you about."

Fifteen minutes later we're curled up on my bed along with Kit and Evelyn. My scream woke them up and thank goodness they're up to speed on all the weird wolfening going on around here. But right now all three of us are staring at Nora like . . . well, like she's turning into a wolf!

"Does it hurt?" Kit asks.

"No," says Nora, scratching the end of her nose. "It's a little wet though."

"That's good," says Evelyn, then after we all look at her,

185

"What? That means she's healthy! Dog's noses are supposed to be wet."

Nora frowns at that. "I think the change has been happening for a few days," she says, explaining her sudden and much fuller armpit hair. "But that's not all. The wolf we saw? I don't think it's a wolf at all. I think it's Jesse!"

"Jesse?" says Evelyn.

"Logan's bunkmate!" I say. "What makes you so sure?"

"They have the same eyes, for one," says Nora. "But it's more than that. I can kind of *feel* it, you know? And he . . ." She trails off, blushing.

"He what?" I ask.

"He smells nice," says Nora sheepishly.

Kit stifles a laugh. "I think someone has a crush."

"On a wolf boy," Evelyn adds.

"There's no time for that now," I say, getting into planning mode. "If Jesse's fully turned into a wolf, and you're on your way, there's definitely something spreading through the camp." I hold up my fingers to count. "Step one, we need to figure out how the wolfening is happening and make sure no one else has been infected."

"But how do we know if someone's started to turn wolfy?" asks Nora. "I didn't notice at first."

"Maybe—" I start, but a sound cuts me off, piercing the otherwise quiet morning. It gives me goose bumps, because I recognize it immediately. By the way the others are looking at me, they do too.

That was a wolf howl.

"Could it be Jesse?" I ask as we all press up against my window, trying to see out.

"It sounded like a *person* howling," says Nora, squished up against me, and even though everything is going wrong and spooky again, I am so happy to have her back on my team.

"Could it be—" Kit starts, but she doesn't finish, because suddenly we see *them*.

It's a dozen campers or so, and two counselors in their matching uniforms. They're running down the path that winds past our cabin, but they're doing it on all fours. The one in front, a kid I recognize as one of the boys from the boathouse, has his tongue flapping out his mouth like a dog's.

Nora gasps. "Big Liam!"

"What are they doing?" Evelyn asks.

"They're chasing that squirrel, look!" Kit says, pointing.

Sure enough, the whole group is chasing after a poor little squirrel who darts up a tree. In a moment, the campers and two counselors are gathered around the base. Big Liam howls—it's the howl we heard before—and the whole pack begins to bark like mad.

"They think they're wolves!" says Nora.

"They don't have any wolf parts though," Kit says. She's right. As far as I can see, everyone looks normal, even if they're behaving like a kennel of hungry dogs.

"Maybe the change is different for everyone," says Nora.

"So how come we haven't gone all doggo?" asks Evelyn. "I mean, I don't *feel* like chasing squirrels."

"Not sure," I say. "But if the whole camp's going wolfy, maybe we need to call for help."

"There's a landline in the main building," says Evelyn. "I got to use it when my mom called about my baby cousin being born."

"Who would we even call?" Kit asks.

I don't actually know. I don't think the FBI has a division to handle werewolves. "Maybe we can figure out how to contact Birdie's society of slayers . . . At the very least, maybe there's something in that office that can help us."

Evelyn nods. "You're right. We'll do some snooping."

"Great," I say, taking charge. "You three should head that way."

"Wait. What do you mean?" says Nora. "Where are you going?"

"I have to go see if Logan is okay," I say. "If we haven't gone totally wolfy, maybe he hasn't either." Nora raises an eyebrow. "Well, at least you're not *acting* like a wolf," I add.

She shakes her head. "No, I mean there's no way you're going after Logan alone."

I want to protest, but Nora grabs my hand and yeah, okay, I really am glad to have her with me.

When the group of wolfed-out campers outside our door loses interest in the squirrel, Nora, Kit, Evelyn, and I sneak out into the morning air. We can hear campers howling and barking in the distance, and even though it sounds friendly, it's more than a little creepy.

"Okay gang," I say to my three friends, my very own pack. "Good luck."

Nora grabs my hand. "Come on," she says. "Time to save the day. Again."

CHAPTER TWENTY-TWO
Nora

"How is it possible that I'm turning into a wolf before I've even had my first kiss?" I groan as Maggie and I make our way through camp. "Life is so unfair sometimes!"

"At least your snout looks kind of cute?" Maggie offers.

I shoot her a look. "Thanks, but I don't believe you one bit. You're my best friend. You have to say that."

"Think of it as your star role. Like Mary Poppins, but wolfy." Maggie's face lights up. "Hairy Poppins!"

I groan and laugh at the same time. "Or El-fur-ba from *Wicked*?"

Maggie snaps her fingers. "Yes! That's good!"

We both erupt into giggles, and it feels nice to be able to make light of something so bizarre. I look around, taking in all the campers who have gone totally feral. Everything is so chaotic no one even notices that I have a literal snout on my face.

"Well . . . at least I'm not alone in this."

"That's for sure." Maggie loops her arm through mine. "And I'm honored to be part of your wolf pack."

"Should we make buttons?" I ask.

"Let's," Maggie agrees.

"There you are!" Logan's voice calls from behind us. We turn around, and he jumps back at the sight of my face. "HOLY—I mean, hello!"

I stand up taller. "What? Haven't you ever seen a girl who's part wolf before?"

He winces. "Sorry. I shouldn't even be surprised since I just saw Hanna Sato chasing Grace Byrne and they were both running on all fours. I didn't even know you could do that! Grace literally climbed a tree carrying Hanna's teddy bear in her mouth like it was a chew toy."

"Impressive," Maggie says.

"I'm glad you guys are okay." Logan's gaze not so subtly darts to my nose. "Well, I mean—"

"I'm fine," I assure him. "Although this snout is seriously sensitive. Everyone here reeks! I really wish Luna hadn't gotten rid of regular deodorant."

Maggie gives me a sympathetic pat on the shoulder. "That's rough." She turns to Logan. "More importantly: we found Jesse!"

Logan's eyes widen. "Are you serious? Where is he?"

"In the woods, I think. He's transformed. Like, fully." When Logan's face goes white, I rush to add, "But he's totally okay! Actually, Claire's been feeding him. I think she might be taking care of him?"

"I have so many questions." Logan's brows knit together. "What do we even do?"

"There's one person who always knows how to deal with weird supernatural stuff. And she also happens to be the first person we saw going wolfy," Maggie says. "Let's go find Birdie."

Along the way to Birdie's cabin, I fill Logan in on my Jesse sighting, the tofu steaks, and Claire's ongoing sneakouts. He is appropriately horrified, but thankful his friend is alive and fine(ish!).

Scattered on the ground outside of Birdie's bunk are the remnants of a recent Sound Bath class, including quartz bowls and mallets; clearly becoming a wolf has made keeping her campsite clean impossible. I get it. I've seen my brothers' rooms.

Maggie yanks on the front door handle, but quickly realizes it's bolted shut with a padlock. "Oh, come on!"

"I have an idea." Logan grabs a mallet from the ground where it had been abandoned. "Stand back."

Maggie and I do. Logan raises the mallet high and smashes it forcefully onto the padlock. It takes a few swings before the lock breaks off. When it does, Logan blinks at it, almost like he hadn't been expecting his plan to work.

"Did that look cool?" he asks. "In my head, that looked cool."

"The coolest," Maggie says, a bit dreamily, and I smile at whatever's happening there. Maybe their time together hasn't only been about the paranormal. "Now, let's go!"

Before we can make a move, Birdie comes crashing out the door—but it's too late. She's already a full-on wolf, just like Jesse! Someone must've locked her in her cabin.

And she's scary. Birdie is huge and agitated and intimidating. Her fur coat ripples as she howls.

Maggie grabs another mallet from the ground and holds it up in front of us. "Birdie! It's *us*!"

Birdie stalks closer, sniffing the ground and snarling the same way Jesse did last night.

"She's hungry!" I blurt.

"Yeah, hungry for humans," Logan says, waving his mallet menacingly at Birdie.

"No, really! I saw Jesse look like this last night and he calmed down after he ate. We need to feed her!" I sniff at the air, desperately hoping there might be a nearby berry bush or some contraband snacks hidden in Birdie's bunk.

With his free hand, Logan reaches into his pocket. "All I have is this." He holds up a bright blue wrapper that reads Nitro Blue Raspberry Cooler–Flavored Edible Non-Food Candy Product. "I bought it at the airport. It's made by some Twitch streamer."

"Give it to Birdie!" Maggie urges.

Logan drops the mallet and rips open the package. He tosses the candy to Birdie, who catches it midair and swallows it in one huge bite.

Instantly, her body transforms. Instead of the hulking wolf we'd just seen, Birdie is now an extremely hairy version of herself—hobbit feet and all.

"Birdie!" Maggie cries. "What's going on?!"

"Maggie?" Birdie frantically looks down at herself and uses her fur-covered human hands to feel her limbs and face, making sure she's really there. Her clothes are a little torn and dirty, but still mostly intact, thankfully, because, oof, that would've been awkward.

"I don't know, but it's bad," Birdie continues. "One second, I was hairy like this and the next I had turned into a wolf! I was so startled, I did the only thing I could think to do: I went to find Luna. I mean, I'd been having weird urges for weeks—wanting to chase squirrels, severe cravings for meat, and hair all over the place. But Luna kept assuring me things were fine. And I believed her! Obviously, things are very much not fine. When she saw I had fully turned, she sweet-talked me back to my cabin and then locked me inside!"

"Jesse turned into a wolf too," Maggie tells her.

"Jesse? He went home to his family. . . ." She shakes her head, and I can see the hurt on her face. "How could she do that to me? To all of us? I trusted her with this place!"

"I'm so sorry, Birdie," I say. Then I take a step closer to her and point to my nose. "I'm turning too."

"Oh, Nora. You poor thing." Birdie frowns. "Is everyone?"

"That's the thing. Some people seem to be fully trans-formed; some are only transforming a little bit." Maggie casts her eyes quickly at me. "Others are acting like wolves but there aren't any physical changes. . . ."

"And some of us seem totally fine," Logan finishes. "For now anyway."

Birdie shakes her head. "Something isn't right. Why are only some of us turning into wolves? And what's causing it in the first place?"

Logan shrugs, hands in the air. "The raw food diet?"

"Everyone would change then, wouldn't they?" I ask.

"That's true," Maggie agrees. She starts to pace. "Hmmm . . ."

"Maybe those words of the day Luna shares over the PA system in the mornings are really spells or hypnosis!" Birdie says suddenly. She crosses her arms. "I should've known. Only a witch could be that enchanting. The witch seminar during my slayer orientation last summer was part of the add-on package. I really should have splurged on that one."

"Wait," Maggie says. "Witches are real too?"

I give Maggie a friendly not-now look and pat Birdie on her fuzzy shoulder. "I don't think that's it," I say as gently as possible.

"Maybe our bodies could each be reacting differently to the food?" Logan offers.

Now I shrug. "I guess that's possible."

Maggie suddenly stops in her tracks. "Birdie, when did

you last fill this up?" She points at a giant overturned bowl at her feet.

"Before dinner last night, why?" Birdie asks.

"It's the moon water, that's why!" Maggie exclaims. "Think about it: It's something we all have access to, but not everyone has been using it the same. Right? Pretty much all the counselors and campers have been drinking it and bathing in it, and, Birdie, you use that stuff more than anyone . . . but we haven't been using it at all!" She motions between herself, Logan, and me.

I clear my throat. "I've maybe been using it a little, which would probably explain the nose."

Logan pumps his fist in the air. "Maggie, you're a genius!"

I shimmy my shoulders in celebration. "My best friend is the smartest person in the world!"

Birdie clucks her tongue. "Not so fast. Weren't you two just part of the slip and slide activity? That was moon water, you know."

Maggie's shoulders slump in defeat. "Oh, that's right."

I hate seeing my friend deflate so quickly And it *has* to be the moon water. Think, Nora, think!

"Well, there must be an antidote, right? Birdie changed back before our very eyes after eating that candy. . . ."

Logan scrunches his nose. "So we all need to eat a Nitro Blue Raspberry Cooler–Flavored Edible Non-Food Candy Product?"

"That, or something like it!" I say excitedly, as I feel the pieces of the puzzle clicking together in my brain. "I don't think the candy itself is the antidote, but the fact that it's a *non-natural product*—the exact thing that's banned from this camp!"

Maggie's face lights up. "I've been secretly using zit cream!" Then she laughs. "Wow, never thought I'd so proudly admit that out loud."

"Wait. So have I, which would explain why we're totally fine, and why the candy helped Birdie!" Logan finishes.

Birdie leaps to her feet and slaps her hands together in triumph. But they're so covered in fur they barely make a sound. "Now that we know, we have to tell the others. I hardly recognized myself after I'd turned. The hunger was all-consuming! If that happens to even a few campers . . . well, let's just say it won't be pretty."

Maggie nods. "We need to be quick about it."

"Where are we going to find enough antidote though?" Logan reaches into his pocket. "I only have one other piece of candy."

There's a twinkle in Birdie's eye. "You're in luck. I helped Luna hide all the contraband we confiscated at the start of camp. Everything's in the barn!"

Maggie, Logan, and I exchange looks. "What are we waiting for? Let's go!"

Birdie shakes her head. "You three go. I'm going to dive into my secret stash of Oreos and wait for some of this hair to dissipate. It's weirdly itchy."

"Meet us at the moon-water pool?" Logan asks.

Birdie gives him a thumbs-up. "You bet."

I arch an eyebrow. "Why the moon-water pool?"

He gives me a devilish grin. "I think it's time we ruin that precious moon water."

Maggie and I break into matching grins. "Absolutely!"

I follow Maggie and Logan before stopping in my tracks. "Actually, wait."

"What's wrong, NorBear?" Maggie asks.

"I'm so sorry, but I have something I need to do first, and I need that last piece of candy in order to do it."

Logan doesn't hesitate and holds it out to me. "You and Maggie are clearly the brains here. Take it."

I close my hand around the candy and look over at Maggie. "I know this sounds really, really shady, and it probably feels like I'm ditching you right now, but I promise—like, I swear on our Broadway dreams and all the Squishmallows in the world and on *Pickle*—this isn't that. I will explain everything when I meet up with you at the moon-water pool in an hour. Do you trust me?"

Maggie smiles. "More than anyone in the world."

CHAPTER TWENTY-THREE
Maggie

Logan and I look at each other the moment we step out onto the path.

"I guess we should have discussed some kind of strategy here for how we were going to get to the barn," I say as a girl from the cabin next to me lifts her leg like she's about to pee on a tree. Thankfully, she doesn't actually.

"Let's just stay calm," he says, his mallet still in his hand. "I don't actually want to use this thing on a fellow camper."

"Yeah, that would be super awkward after they de-wolfed. Like, hey, sorry about the black eye. I thought you were going to turn me into a chew toy."

"Um, my friend's older brother Chandler teaches dog training classes at PetSmart and he always says two things. First: there are no bad dogs, only bad owners."

A guy with shaggy brown hair who sometimes sits with us at lunch and just repeats everyone's jokes, but louder, is restlessly circling a patch of grass and then throwing his body down on the ground and rolling around before getting back up again and circling in search of the perfect spot. "I really hope the other thing Chandler always says is more helpful."

Logan nods. "The second thing he always says is that dogs are more likely to chase you if you run."

"So no running?" I ask.

"Cool and calm," he says as we slowly make our way up the path.

"But dogs can smell fear though, right? And they have, like, heightened senses or something, so they can probably hear my heart beating out of my chest too. Do they want to lick us or eat us or what?"

A girl from my primal scream workshop with a brutal sunburn is on all fours and uses the trunk of a tree to scratch her butt.

"Let's just keep an eye out for any vicious behavior," Logan tells me.

This is fine, I tell myself over and over again as I walk carefully over the gravel, trying not to make too much noise.

With the barn just up the hill and in sight, one of the Big Liams steps out onto the path. He's on all fours as he stalks over to us, drool dripping from his snarled lips.

"Who's a good boy?" I squeak.

Sweat begins to roll down Logan's temple as the grip on his mallet tightens and that's when I know things are no longer cool or calm.

"Run?" I ask him.

He nods. "As fast as you can!"

We sprint past Big Liam and his jaw snaps at my heels . . . followed by something wet. Ew! Seriously? Did Big Liam just lick me? Gross!

Adrenaline drives me up the hill and I don't even have time to panic over whether the barn is even unlocked. But thankfully it's open and the moment Logan slides the door shut behind me, paws—no hands!—bang up against the door.

The two of us peek out the dusty covered window to see a whole pack of campers have chased us up the hill with both of the Big Liams leading the way. They're all in different stages of wolfening. Some are still on two legs while others are on all four. There are those that look sweet and harmless enough to rescue from an animal shelter and then there are a few like the Big Liams who look like they could bite hard enough to crush bone.

"How are we going to get out of here?" Logan asks.

"That's a problem for Maggie and Logan ten minutes from now," I tell him before—*gulp*—grabbing his hand and tugging him toward the locked cabinets on the far wall. "Right now, we gotta find that contraband."

"I hope Birdie was right," he says. "Luna was dumping everything in trash bags when she did her sweep."

"Luna doesn't strike me as the type to dump this all in a landfill or something. You ready to use that mallet?"

"Oh yeah," he says. "Stand back."

I do and then watch as he strikes the first cabinet a few

times until the wood splinters and the padlock clinks on to the floor.

"Whoa," we both say in unison.

"And this is just the first cabinet," I say as I pull out my backpack and carefully remove my EMF reader. I should leave it here for safekeeping and hope some half-wolf kid doesn't decide to play fetch with it because the priority is contraband for the moon water. "Let's get as much as we can in here."

The first cabinet alone is stuffed with the kind of candies that are 50 percent food dye and high fructose corn syrup. There are face washes and prescription strength deodorant and pimple patches and makeup and glitter hair gel and even some energy drinks. It's like a pharmacy and convenience store smushed into four little cabinets. A proverbial smorgasbord of everything Luna stands against.

When my bag is full, Logan dumps out a basket of painted rocks labeled *Pet rocks because rocks are friends. Take one*. He begins to fill the basket with what we hope will be the antidote to the collective wolf-out happening outside. "I really thought this would just be a normal summer at camp," he mutters. "First werewolves. Now pet rocks."

"The pet rocks really sent you over the edge, huh? The fact that there isn't even a full moon right now is so weird. And it's daytime! I guess some of that werewolf stuff is a myth."

"Sylvia broke a few vampire myths, too, so there's no telling what's fact or fiction," he says.

After a few minutes, we stand there with my backpack,

his basket, and our pockets stuffed. Outside, campers are scratching at the doors and windows and the creep factor is nearly at maximum capacity.

"We can't get out of here," I say.

Logan plops down on the floor. "We'll just have to wait them out. They'll get distracted by something else eventually. A bird, the mail carrier . . . something!"

I sit down next to him so that we're both out of view of the windows. Maybe the other campers will forget we're even in here.

"I can't believe Birdie fell for Luna's bogus philosophies. I mean, this all-natural stuff isn't all bad, but at the risk of turning everyone into werewolves . . . what was Birdie thinking? She had to know something was up," I say.

"Crushes make you do silly things," he says, like he knows something about crushes. "People don't act right when they're crushing on someone. I mean, usually it's harmless. Cute, even! But not when your crush is turning a whole camp into a pack of werewolves and you can't see past how perfect you think they are."

I turn my head so he can't see the way my cheeks turn pink. "Well, thankfully I haven't had a crush on any evil villains."

"Yeah, me neither," he says. "Just regular old awesome people for me."

Awesome people like who, I wonder. My heart races a little at the thought of being one of those awesome people.

Outside, the camp-wide speakers crackle to life. Maybe it's Luna giving her army of half wolves some kind of command or maybe—

"Coming to you live this morning," says a staticky radio voice, "and this next song is a flashback to 2010. 'Howlin' for You' by the Black Keys."

"That's weird," I mumble. "I didn't think Luna liked music that didn't involve moaning or gongs."

"A-baby," the song croons. *"I'm howlin' for you."*

Logan chuckles. "My uncle loves this song."

"Feels a little too literal right now," I say dryly.

But Logan doesn't seem to mind the freakishly on-point lyrics as he hops up and holds a hand out for me. "Come on."

"We can't go out there yet," I tell him.

"No, I mean come on and dance with me, Maggie!" He grins and my stomach turns to lava.

I comb through every reason in my head to tell him no. We're supposed to be helping all our fellow campers from fully wolfing out. What if I step on his toes? I've only been good at dancing when it's choreographed like in a musical.

"The dance is basically canceled now," he says. "And we didn't even get to dance together!"

The bubbling in my stomach stops just long enough for me to realize how much I was really looking forward to the ball . . . and to dancing . . . with Logan.

I take his hand and stand. Even though the song is a little fast and even though I've literally never heard it in my life,

Logan puts his hand on my waist and I place my hand on his shoulder, our other hands clasped together.

Do they make deodorant for palms? Because mine are producing some serious sweat at the moment.

I follow Logan's lead as we dance in circles around the barn for a minute before just swaying to the music.

I want to be brave. I want to so badly. I want to be the kind of person who doesn't care about letting a primal scream rip through her lungs without feeling silly or dance with her arms flailing like every emotion in her body can be interpreted through movement. This is my chance. This is my chance to howl at the moon and tell Logan the truth about how I feel.

"I like you," I blurt.

"Back atcha, Maggie," he says cooly.

I stop swaying. Either I'm getting motion sickness or this whole spilling-my-guts thing is making me queasy. "No. Um. Logan, I like you as more than a friend."

His eyes are wide and unblinking. I wish I could scoop the words back into my mouth, but it's too late.

"I didn't realize it at first. Or maybe I liked you as a friend and then more than that later on. My mom always says the best relationships start as friendships." I'm blabbering. A relationship? What am I even talking about? "I'm just trying to—"

"Maggie," he says before leaning forward and giving me a soft kiss on the cheek.

I gasp as my stomach drops to the floor.

"I like you too," he says, the apples of his cheeks turning pink. "The same way you like me."

"You—you do?" I manage to ask through my absolute astonishment. Goose bumps run up my arms, and it's not even because I'm kind of fearing for our lives here.

Suddenly the camp speakers crackle again and the song stops abruptly, only for the sound of incessant barking to take over. "And that's why your furry best friend deserves a vacation at Puppy Paradise next time you and your family say bon voyage." The barking on the radio commercial continues before abruptly switching to some classical song and then to a sportscaster calling the play-by-play of a baseball game.

"Howie," I gasp as I regretfully pull away from Logan and run to the nearest window. The campers are . . . gone. They've all run off to the various speakers and are barking and pawing up at them.

"He created a distraction!" Logan says in awe.

"We have to go," I say as we both jog over to the big barn door. "We've got some moon water to ruin!"

Note to self: Does a kiss on the cheek count as a first kiss? Must confer with Nora.

After we save the whole camp, of course.

Again.

CHAPTER TWENTY-FOUR
Nora

Now that we know there's an antidote to this whole wolf thing, I have to find Jesse. He's been stuck in wolf form the longest of us all, and if a piece of candy could turn him back (even a little), then I have to help.

I head back to my cabin, trying to act as casual as possible for a girl who's surrounded by half wolves, half humans. When I arrive, the door is wide open, which is not a good sign. I have no idea what I'll find in there and I kind of wish I'd taken that mallet with me.

From inside comes the now-familiar sound of a wolf growling, followed by a human whimper. Claire!

Before I can think too hard about how I'm still mad at her, I burst inside. A terrified Claire is perched on top of her dresser, and growling at her from the floor is Jesse the Wolf—and he looks *mad*. He snarls at her, drool dripping from his mouth. He looks about ready to take a bite out of her.

"Nora!" Claire cries when she spots me.

"Oh, hey, Claire," I say, keeping my voice cool. "Did you run out of I Can't Believe It's Not Steak!?"

"Please get that thing away from me!" She tears her gaze away from Jesse, then her face twists in horror as she takes in the sight of me. "Actually, you can both just stay away from me!"

Jesse the Wolf lets out a low growl, baring his teeth at Claire.

I scowl at her, too, though I doubt I look half as menacing. "He's not a thing—he's Jesse, and you know it. And I'm not going anywhere. This is my bunk too!"

Claire pulls her knees closer to her chest in a desperate attempt to get away. "Okay, okay, I'm sorry. Just—don't hurt me!"

I flip my hair over my shoulder. "I wouldn't waste my energy." Then I turn to Jesse and I reach into the front pocket of my floral overalls and pull out the Nitro Blue Raspberry Cooler–Flavored Edible Non-Food Candy Product from Logan.

"Jesse," I coo in a voice I would use on an adorable baby. "Brought you something. You must be starving."

At the sight of the food, Jesse bounds over to me, tail wagging.

I rip open the snack and he eats it right from my hand. Like Birdie, Jesse swallows it in one gulp, and quickly transforms from a four-legged furry wolf into a two-legged hairy boy with mismatched eyes. He's not cured by any means, but for now, it's enough.

"Jesse!" I breathe a sigh of relief. "Are you okay?"

He blinks a few times, staring down at his hands (not paws!) like this is the first time he's seeing them. Considering he's been in wolf form for almost two weeks, his clothes are way dirtier than Birdie's, but still covering enough of him that I don't have to look away.

"I'm honestly not sure. . . ." he admits.

"Is he back to normal? How?" Claire asks, slowly climbing down from the dresser. She keeps her distance, as if not wanting to get too close to either one of us.

"Not yet, but he will be. It was the candy. We're guessing synthetic things might be the key to changing people back into themselves, but I don't know." I bite my lip, motioning toward my snout. "I'm still not exactly sure how this all works. I mean, look at me."

Jesse's mouth quirks up into a half grin as he scratches his arms. "What, that ol' thing? Barely noticeable." He twitches his own snout at me, which makes me laugh.

"Well, what *do* you know?" Claire presses. "Everyone is running around like they've gone totally bananas! I knew my mom never should've done that stupid slip and slide. It got that cursed moon water on us all!"

I turn and narrow my eyes. "Is transforming into a *werewolf* one of the 'harmless side effects' your mom was talking about a few days ago?"

She winces. "I think so."

"And you didn't tell me? Or anyone?" I demand.

"I didn't know, I swear! Not until—" Claire's eyes flit to Jesse.

Jesse glares at her. "She pushed me into the moon-water bath."

My jaw drops. "She did what?! What is *wrong* with you?"

"I swear I had no idea the moon water would turn Jesse into a wolf!" Claire protests. "My mom knew that its healing properties came with side effects, but never told anyone what they were—I was just trying to see what they were and hopefully put a stop to her forcing moon water on everyone."

"So you used me as a test subject? You could've tried it on yourself!" Jesse's voice is dripping with anger. "Unbelievable."

"Anything could've happened to Jesse! Not to mention you knew the moon water really did have healing properties, but you insisted it was all just vitamins and tricks of the light." I shake my head. "You put Jesse at serious risk and you lied to all of us!"

"I was trying to help! I thought if I made the moon water sound less appealing to everyone, people wouldn't bother using it. I didn't know my mom planned to infuse the water into everything, and I definitely didn't know it could turn people into werewolves!" Claire's eyes start to water as she talks. "My whole life, my mom's been dedicated to using crystals and natural healing. She was convinced that it was the key to happiness for everyone, especially because it brought her peace after she had such a rough time growing up. When she realized moon water could 'fix imperfections,' she became obsessed with getting it into the hands of as many people as possible. She said she wanted to save people from the pain of being bullied for their looks, like she had been growing up. But the moon water is clearly not safe! My mom didn't care though. No matter how often I pleaded with her to let go of the moon water all together, she refused. She wouldn't tell me what the side effects were and I got desperate. I decided to take things into my own hands. I thought if I could prove there are side effects from the moon water, I could save everyone from it and expose my mom for who she really is. Instead, I just turned Jesse into a wolf."

"You left me that way for a *week* without telling a soul," Jesse finishes. "I get that you wanted to help people, Claire, but there were better ways."

My head is spinning with all this information, so much so that I need to sit down. I sink onto my bed, rubbing my temples and trying to process.

I'm furious with Claire for what she did to Jesse. There is no excuse! Even if she meant well, she put him in a really unsafe situation, which in turn put us ALL in unsafe situations. What if we hadn't figured out there was an antidote? Would we all be stuck as werewolves forever?

Yet I can also hear the desperation in her voice. I believe her when she says she was trying to help, and I can't imagine having such a difficult relationship with your own mom, someone who you're supposed to be able to trust and rely on. It doesn't make any of this okay, but it does help me understand her a little more.

And Luna? How could she let us all use this moon water when she suspected something wasn't right? How much did she know, exactly? And why can't she accept that physical differences aren't flaws that need fixing?

"We need to undo this huge mess before anyone else turns," I say finally. "And, as much as I hate to admit it, I think that means talking to your mom. She needs to be stopped."

Jesse nods. "Being a wolf sucks. Trust me. I don't want that for anyone else, if we can help it."

"Did you hear anything I just said? She won't listen to me," Claire argues. "She only cares about her precious moon water!"

"She'll listen if you make her," I say. "If *we* make her."

"Yeah," Jesse adds. "We'll all talk to her. Together."

Claire's face softens. "Really? You'll help me? Even after what I did?"

Jesse sighs. "Yeah. Even after what you did."

I give Jesse a soft smile, touched by his generosity in spite of all Claire has put him through. I turn to Claire. "And, after we figure this whole wolf mess out, I think . . . maybe you should talk to her about how she treats you too. You deserve better."

There's a pause, and I half expect Claire to start arguing with me. To my surprise, though, she pulls me into a huge, emotional hug.

"Thank you," she whispers. "And I'm so sorry—for everything. The stress has been getting to me and I've been lashing out. But I really do like you, Nora. I hope we can still be friends."

I hug Claire back. "We'll figure it out."

It's the best I can offer right now. Even though I understand Claire better now, it doesn't excuse what she did. Also: she is kinda the reason I'm part werewolf right now. Not cool.

"Okay," Claire says with a sniffle.

I pull back from the hug. "For now, I think we've got bigger things to worry about. I'd love to get this all fixed before I start sprouting wolf ears."

"Are you saying my wolf ears aren't adorable?" Jesse asks, pretending to be hurt.

"Well, yours are, obviously. It's just everyone else I worry about." I grin. "Now, come on. I'm supposed to meet up with Logan and Maggie at the moon-water pool so we can fix this mess."

"Fine," sighs Jesse. "Just keep Claire far, far away from me."

Claire sticks out her tongue at him, and we all burst into much-needed laughter.

CHAPTER TWENTY-FIVE
Maggie

Logan and I rush over to the moon-water pool while Howie distracts the other campers.

Instead of stressing out about one of them suddenly lunging at us, I am deeply embarrassed by the memory of just moments ago when I told Logan I *like* like him.

I mean, he did kiss me on the cheek, so he *like* likes me too, but why do I still feel like my face is on fire? But I'm also absolutely giddy. Add this to the list of things I must dissect with Nora once we've hopefully de-wolfed this place.

"Jesse?" Logan says the moment the moon-water pool is in sight. He takes off running and it takes a moment for my brain to catch up and realize—holy heck—that really is Jesse standing there with Nora and . . . ugh, Claire.

I run after him down the hill and watch as he collides with his friend.

"Uh, bro, you're a lot hairier than I remember," Logan tells him.

"Yeah, well you turn into a wolf at summer camp and there are gonna be some side effects," Jesse says. His ears are still in sharp hairy points and fur is bunching out of his clothing like it's trying to escape.

Logan's eyes bug out as he shakes his head. "I have so many questions."

"We don't really have time for that," Nora says.

"I just want to know how Jesse turned into a werewolf to begin with," I tell her.

Claire opens her mouth to speak, but Nora touches her arm to stop her. "It's a long story and one we will totally get to later."

I eye them both suspiciously, trying not to be annoyed with Claire, who is giving off some unusually nice vibes. I almost want to ask if she's okay or if this is just part of her plan to steal my BFF right out from under my nose.

"If we want things to get back to normal around here, we've got some moon water to spoil," Logan says as he puts his basket on the floor and drops into a squat.

I follow his lead and unzip my backpack after giving Claire a solid I've-got-my-eye-on-you look. I want to just forget about the last week and how she went out of her way to make me look like a loser and also scoop Nora from me, but sometimes I hold on to a grudge as tight as a bucket of popcorn during a scary movie.

Which is exactly why I need to just get over myself. Since I'm so suddenly evolved, I look up to Claire and smile, hoping

I don't look as wonky as I feel.

"You guys really made out with tons of contraband," Nora says.

"There's even more where that came from," Logan tells her. "The whole barn is—"

"Stop!" a voice rings out and even the distracted wolfy campers momentarily freeze.

Luna comes barreling down the hill and flings her body over the moon-water bath so that she's blocking it from us. "You can't contaminate the water with that—that rubbish! You'll ruin everything!"

"*We'll* ruin everything?" I ask her. "Your little miracle moon water has turned most of the campers into tween wolves! You're barking up the wrong tree, lady!"

Logan and Jesse start to pry her off the bath and her knuckles turn white from holding on so tight. Jesse growls at her, and Logan grunts.

Claire sulks back behind Nora, like her mom is making her feel suddenly small and oh, how I can relate.

"Don't you see what's happening?" I ask her. "What are you going to do when all these kids turn into wolves and eventually they can't turn back? Look what you've already done to Jesse and Birdie!"

"We haven't even had a full moon yet," Nora tells her. "And I may not know much about full moons, but I'm pretty sure those are kind of a big deal."

"I never meant for this to happen," Luna says, her grip

only slightly loosening. "I was only trying to save you all from the pains of growing up. My teen and pre-teen years were miserable. Acne, painful braces, uncontrollable hormones. I didn't even want to get out of bed in the morning." She turns back to Claire. "I couldn't bear the thought of that happening to you, Claire. Or anyone else for that matter. I haven't always been the best mom to you, honey, and I only have you for the summers. But you have to believe me. I did this for you. I—I thought I could make growing up easier for you." She turns back to the rest of us. "For all of you."

Claire's eyes are watery with tears, and she looks so confused.

"How does turning me into a werewolf help anyone?" Jesse asks, his voice full of anger. "Forget acne or my voice cracking. I have enough body hair to survive with polar bears right now."

Luna stands up, giving up her guard on the moon-water tub and turns to Jesse. "I didn't turn you into a werewolf, Jesse. None of you have been exposed to enough moon water to fully turn. There's something else going on here. I don't know for sure, but—"

"I pushed Jesse into the moon-water bath," Claire blurts.

I gasp. "What?"

Nora cringes a little bit. "We don't really have time for this right now."

"Claire, certainly that's not true." Luna shakes her head in disbelief. "Surely it's not that strong." She turns to her daughter, and here with them side by side, it's much easier to look past their differences and see how alike they look despite how differently they act and dress. Their long, long limbs and snowy skin. The straight, narrow noses they both seem to share. "Claire, honey, why would you do such a thing?"

Claire throws up her arms, sputtering. "Because I wanted to prove once and for all that all this hokey stuff you're into is bogus. But I guess it turns out that this one thing is way too real for your own good!" She turns back to Jesse. "Again, I really am sorry."

"So I thought if I pushed someone in, I'd expose you," Claire continues. "But that all backfired on me. Thankfully, Maggie, Nora, and Logan figured out an antidote."

"Yeah," I chime in, "and it involves making a big goopy moon-water stew, so if you don't mind, we have some campers to help. If a little piece of candy can reverse some of the effects, then maybe dumping this contraband in the moon water and dousing as many infected campers as we can will fix all this mess."

Luna wrings her hands nervously. "I just . . . I was so close. I'm really on to something."

Nora steps forward with her hands on her hips. "Maybe if you really want to be on to something, you should make things right with Claire and help us fix this whole mess."

Three campers gallop past us on all fours chasing a squirrel down to the lake.

Luna sighs. The braid that makes a crown around her head is messy and sweaty.

"Wait a minute," I say. "If you're such a fan of your moon water, why haven't you wolfed out yet?"

Logan crosses his arms, all the contraband piled up around our feet. "You must not be fully committed to your all-natural lifestyle, Luna."

Claire smirks. "Tell them, Mom."

"From time to time, I get . . . Botox. It's just a silly little injection that stops your face from getting wrinkly." She turns to Claire. "And I may have tried some under eye patches I confiscated from a camper."

"See?" Claire says. "A total fraud."

Luna nods sadly. "I deserve that. I really do. Claire, I'm so sorry. I should know better than to think I could protect you from the pains of growing up. I just thought if I could fix this one thing for you, I would make up for all the times I haven't been there." She looks over at the rest of us as we watch this moment that feels too personal. "I'm sorry to all of you. I wanted to turn this place into a refuge for you all, but instead I made this summer a nightmare."

"You're really sorry?" Claire whispers.

Luna holds an arm out for her daughter, who crashes into her.

Another camper darts past us chasing a volleyball down the hill and Luna wipes at the tears she's begun to spill. "Okay, okay, let's make this right."

Claire half smiles and Nora lets out a deep breath. All of us are itching to dig through the supplies Logan and I brought down from the barn. Luna's nose wrinkles at the sight of it all, but she still helps and begins to unwrap candy and remove safety seals from tubes and jars.

I reach for a bag of extra sour Warheads and, because what better thing to dump into the tub first than the most atomically sour candy ever?

As I stand, Claire steps past Nora toward me. "Maggie," she starts, "I just wanted to say how sorry—"

Her foot catches on a rock and she trips forward, falling right into me.

I drop the bag of Warheads on the ground and reach out to catch her, but she knocks me off-balance and before I can catch myself, I'm tipping backward and directly into the tub of moon water.

The moment my body hits the surface, I feel warm and safe like when your shoulders are under the water in a pool on a chilly summer night. But then just a second later, my vision begins to blur as I hear the sound of bones cracking. Every bit of me burns right down to my fingertips and the last thing I hear is Nora screaming my name.

CHAPTER TWENTY-SIX
Nora

How could we have been so close to fixing everything and then, POOF?

One wrong move from Claire and I'm forced to watch as my best friend turns into a wolf right before my eyes. I'd seen the opposite before—wolf to human—but never the other way around.

It's creepy, actually, how simultaneously fast and slow the transformation happens: Maggie's limbs stretch as hair sprouts from her skin like those sped-up videos of flowers blooming from the soil; her hands and feet spread into gigantic paws with sharp nails; and her sweet face goes beastly, complete with a long snout, pointy ears, and fanged teeth.

As soon as Maggie changes into a wolf, she bolts away fast as lightning, and all I'm left with is the pit of anger in my stomach directed right at Claire.

How could she do this? It seems she didn't learn her lesson at all, even after Jesse, and now she's gone and messed with the wrong person: my best friend.

"I can't believe you!" I hiss, my fists balling at my side.

Claire's eyes are round as saucers. "Oh my gosh! It was an accident. I swear!"

My nostrils flare as I glare at her. "Does it matter? Maggie is a wolf thanks to you!"

Someone reaches out to touch my elbow and when I turn, it's Jesse. "She'll be okay. We just need to find her."

He's right. Jesse had been fully transformed into a wolf for over a week and it only took one small piece of candy to bring him back.

Luna steps forward with her hand barely raised. "Actually . . . the moon water is much more potent than it was at the beginning of camp. The moon has been charging it each night. We can't be sure of what we're dealing with here."

I take a deep breath in and let it out. "We have to try, but first, I have to go find her."

"No way," Logan argues. "Have you seen the way everyone has been acting? It's not safe out there alone! I'll go with you."

Claire nods. "Seriously, Nora. Don't do this! What if you run into a wolf that's hungry?" She swallows hard. "They can be scary when they're hungry. Trust me."

"It has to be me," I say firmly. "My senses are already heightened, and I was the only one who could connect with Jesse when he was in wolf form. I might as well put this snout to good use. I can track her down the fastest. We're best friends." I look at Claire as I emphasize that last part, which might be a little mean, but she did just push Maggie into the moon-water bath.

If I were Maggie, where would I go?

I sniff around, hoping I might catch her scent. If we weren't at camp, I could easily track her down from the fruity perfume she usually wears (I bought it for her for Christmas because it came in the cutest pink bottle shaped like a teddy bear). But because Luna made us go all natural, I have to rely on what I know about Maggie instead.

There's no way she would've run into camp based on how chaotic it was. She could go to the abandoned boathouse, I guess, but that place has become more of a hangout for me and Claire than for Maggie. She might run wildly into the woods without a plan, but that doesn't really feel like Maggie either. Maggie always has a plan, and it's one of the things I admire most about her.

And Maggie's plan this summer was to investigate the campgrounds with her EMF reader!

"The EMF reader," I say. "Do you think it can pick up werewolf activity?" I ask.

"*Great* minds." Logan shrugs off a backpack I hadn't noticed him wearing, reaches in to get something, then triumphantly hands me the device. "I grabbed it as soon as I saw it in the barn. Just in case!"

I hit the switch on the side of the detector and it buzzes to life as lights on the small screen begin to flicker.

"It's like a metal detector for the paranormal." Logan smiles. "You got this. Just be careful and bring back our Maggie."

Without waiting for anyone else to weigh in, I take off running in the same direction as Maggie. Never thought I'd say this, but there is a small part of me that thinks I could totally find her faster if I could run on all fours the way the other campers have been.

I run alongside the lake for a minute, but the EMF reader isn't lighting up, so I veer up the hill and suddenly, I've got beeping and yellow lights.

I must be getting closer . . . to something, and I certainly hope it's Maggie and not some angry ghost—or another wolfed-out camper. As I run past the barn, the reader starts going haywire. I'm getting closer!

I book it in the direction of Captain B's bunk, and there's no doubt that there's something out here. *Please be Maggie.*

The door to her cabin is wide open, so I walk inside.

"Hello?" I call out, my adrenaline pumping. "Howie, if this is you, I'm totally okay with you just ignoring me . . . Maggie, are you in here?"

A soft whine comes from the corner of the room.

I let out a relieved sigh when I spot a wolf with a friend-ship bracelet—*our* friendship bracelet—tangled around its paw as it hides under a blanket on Birdie's bed.

"Maggie!" I rush over to the bed and try to pull the blanket off her head, but she lets out a little growl and tugs on it

224

with her mouth. "Maggie? That is you, right?" I hold up my wrist to her paw, putting our matching bracelets side by side. "Otherwise, I've somehow managed to wear the exact same bracelet as a wild wolf, and that's a fashion faux pas I might never get over. . . ."

Maggie lets out some air from her nose—my best guess is that's her wolfish attempt at a laugh?—but she still doesn't come out.

I crouch down beside the bed and reach for the blanket. Maggie lets out a tiny whimper.

"Do you not want me to see you?" I ask softly.

Beneath the blanket, she shakes her head from side to side.

"Oh, Magpie." I shrug off the denim button-up I'd been wearing over my overalls and tank top and tie the shirt around my waist. "So, even though it looks cute, I wasn't wearing this shirt because of my amazing sense of fashion. I was trying to hide some of the body hair that's been growing since I started using moon water. Look."

Maggie's grayish blue eyes peek out from beneath the blanket and focus in on my hairy armpits.

"See? I gave up on shaving them after I broke one of Claire's disposable razors. And, you know, it's not actually that bad now that I've left it alone. Mami always says anyone who has a problem with girls having body hair isn't worth our time anyway." I smile, even though I'm not sure she can see it. "Can you come out now?"

Ever so slowly, I watch as the blanket covering Maggie falls to the bed, revealing Maggie in her full wolf form. With her ears tucked back and her eyes as big as saucers, she looks more like a sweet dog than a ferocious werewolf. "There's my bestie. I'm really sorry this happened. Claire swears it was an accident."

Maggie growls, and I don't blame her. Then her ears perk.

"Do you hear something?" I ask.

She leaps off the bed in one fluid motion and bounds toward the door. For a second, I worry another camper has fully transformed and they might be hungry—but I'm relieved to see Jesse and Birdie at the door. They're both more wolf than human at this point, which makes me think the antidote in small doses must work only temporarily.

Jesse, Birdie, and Maggie exchange a series of sniffs and whines, then Birdie lets out one long howl. I'm not transformed enough to know exactly what they're saying, but I know one thing: when a wolf howls, it's like a rallying cry to assemble the pack.

I nod at Birdie. "My thoughts exactly. Let's do this!"

She leads the way toward the moon-water pool, Jesse and Maggie turning to check on me every few steps to make sure I'm still with them. Once again, here I am cursed with just two legs, and we've got some serious ground to cover!

We end up back at the moon-water bath minutes later to find that the water has gone from glittering and iridescent to murky and bubbling, chock-full of random items like silly string, marshmallow fluff, and sunblock. Logan is even squeezing some zit cream into the water when we arrive.

"You've been busy!" I say to him.

Logan looks up and wipes a bead of sweat from his forehead. "Yeah! Did you find Maggie?"

Claire stands beside him and Luna looks on hopefully as she paces behind them.

Maggie is crouched behind Jesse and Birdie, hiding.

I nod. "She's okay. Is this ready?"

"I think so?" Logan's voice goes up in a question. "I mean, I've never had to make a massive wolf antidote before, so I don't know."

"Only one way to find out." I walk over to Maggie, patting her on the back, and whisper, "You ready?"

She looks at the pool and gives me a whimper. The water is, quite frankly, disgusting, so this is probably the most enthusiastic yes I'm going to get.

"Can everyone, maybe, turn around? Let's give our friends some privacy," I say.

Logan immediately puts his back to us. "Of course."

"Gladly," Claire agrees, twirling around.

Luna claps her hands over her eyes. "I can't watch this anyway."

I turn too. "Okay, you guys. On three. One . . . two . . . three!"

Then I hear the sound of splashing. I hold my breath, and I wait.

CHAPTER TWENTY-SEVEN
Maggie

I sit on the ground staring at my hands—the same hands that were paws just moments ago. My whole body trembles as Nora crushes into me.

"Maggie! Oh my gosh! You're okay!"

I think she's telling herself just as much as she is telling me.

"Maggie, say something," she says.

I look up and Jesse and Birdie are there hovering over us.

"Whoa," I finally manage to say. "Did that really just happen?"

Jesse holds his hand out to pull Nora up and Birdie does the same for me.

"Yeah, kid," Birdie says. "It really did, and luckily your best friend here saved the day before you could disappear into the woods without a trace."

My eyes immediately burn with tears, my heart swelling. "I can't believe you did that for me, NorBear."

She nods. "Don't sound so surprised. I'd do anything for you."

Now it's me who's tackling her with a hug.

"This is a really touching moment," Jesse says. "Like, seriously, it's giving me all the feels, but we sort of need to figure out how to save the rest of the campers."

Birdie nods. "I don't think we can really wrangle everyone and dunk them in moon water."

My head hurts from transforming and trying to problem-solve makes everything throb. "I just wish there was a way we could bring the moon water to them, ya know?"

"I knew I should have packed my super soaker," Jesse mumbles.

Birdie's eyes light up and she takes off into the trees. "Follow me."

The four of us sneak past a pack of campers roughhousing with each other on all fours and into the barn.

"Maggie and Logan already cleared this place out," Nora says as Birdie closes the door behind us.

"No, they didn't," Birdie says confidently as she steps onto the stage and opens a small trap door. "I should've thought of it sooner, but I almost forgot this was here."

The three of us step to the edge of the hole in the floor and right there inside the stage are stacks of balloons and water guns. Now, this is what I'd hoped to find at summer camp.

"I stocked up last summer when I thought I could take Sylvia out with holy water, but then I ended up not using any of this stuff and I thought I'd just save it for camp this summer. But I didn't think Luna would go for the balloons or the plastic on the water guns," Birdie explains.

"This is perfect," I tell her. "Let's take as much as we can carry."

"Maggie," Evelyn and Kit squeak excitedly as they see me walking down the hill with my arms full.

Logan walks to meet me. We're all still trying to avoid making too much noise or running, but my stomach tickles as he reaches me and takes half my load of supplies from me. With one arm, he hugs me and says, "I'm so glad you're back on two legs."

"Me too," I tell him.

"Are these water guns for what I think they're for?" he asks hopefully.

"Yeah, they are," Jesse chimes in as he, Nora, and Birdie join us.

At the moon-water pool, Kit, Evelyn, Claire, and Luna are waiting.

Evelyn takes one look at us with the pile of water guns and balloons. "Bloody genius," she declares.

Luna opens her mouth to say something about toxins or plastic or something, I'm sure, but Claire elbows her in the ribs. "How can I help?" she says a second later.

Nora takes charge and organizes us all into a line as we work together to fill the water guns and balloons, making a quick task of it.

"This is great," Birdie says as she surveys our work. "Let's split off into groups and have a moon-water war. What do ya say?"

"I say let's kick some werewolf butt," Claire says. She hands her mom a neon-yellow water gun along with a handful of balloons. "Come on, Mom!"

She and Luna stalk off up the hill while Nora and Jesse pair up and Birdie, Evelyn, and Kit set off in the other direction.

"How's your aim?" I ask Logan.

He holds the water gun up, ready for action. "Let's just say that despite what my mom thinks, video games are good for something."

We take off toward the water where a group of campers are pawing around on the shore.

Logan and I sneak up on them. He aims and begins to pump water at them as I use a slingshot to launch water balloons at anyone he misses.

And one by one, campers return to themselves. A little confused, for sure, but it's working!

We even track down both Big Liams, who are being teased by a couple of mischievous birds, though I have to admit there's not much difference between the wolfed-out and human versions of those two.

And I might have thrown one or two more water balloons at them than I needed to. . . .

Just to be sure, of course!

As Nora and I stand to walk over to the compost bin to throw away our breakfast food scraps, one of the Big Liams lets out a whining growl as he eyes the half-eaten vegan sausage on my tray.

I hold it out for him and he stabs it with his knife before scarfing it down in one bite.

It's been three days since the whole camp wolfed out and went wild, and even though everyone is fully human again, all of us who transformed in some ways are still sporting a few side effects. In my case, my nails are only just now starting to dull, and my ears are still bushy with hair sprouting from the inside. Maybe when I get home, I can dig up my dad's nose hair trimmer to see if it will help.

None of the kids really remember what happened, and to anyone who's asked, Luna has blamed the very fuzzy memory of that day on a full sugar and fructose syrup heavy meal that was accidentally served in the cafeteria.

Nora's still battling her armpit hair, but she doesn't seem to actually mind it too much and even went swimming without her T-shirt yesterday.

"I can't believe it's the last day," I tell Nora as we walk outside and back down toward the cabins so we can each pack up to go home.

"I'm ready to go home," she says, "but this also means our summer is half over, which is not cool. I'm not ready for eighth grade!"

I wave her off. "We survived werewolf camp. Eighth grade is going to be easier than the time we beat your brothers in the New Year's Eve Bananagrams tournament."

She loops her arm through mine and leans her head on my shoulder. "I'll have you and that's all that matters. Hey, do you think my armpit hair will chill out before the first day?"

"Maybe, but it's okay if it doesn't. Forget going back to middle school with perfectly shaved legs or pits or suddenly big boobs! We can officially say we've transformed into wolves and back over summer break. We basically mastered the art of puberty if you ask me."

"That's a good way of looking at it," Nora agrees.

We stop for a moment outside of Nora and Claire's cabin and sit on a huge stump as we watch parents start to park their cars and venture out onto the campgrounds.

Down by the lake, the once full and glittering moon-water tub is empty and shockingly plain looking.

"Birdie says Luna dumped the moon water into the lake," I tell Nora.

"Does that mean Lake of the Ozarks is going to be full of werefish?"

"Huh . . . I hadn't thought of that, but I think we're safe."

Nora crosses her arms over her chest. "Do you really think she poured it all out though? How do we know she didn't save some for herself to replicate or something? Sylvia wanted to start a beverage empire. Maybe Luna's willing to sell her soul to the skin-care gods."

"Well, that would be straight-up diabolical," I say. "But she did seem really sorry, and she did let everyone get all their stuff back—or what was left of it at least. I really missed regular bug spray."

"Ugh, me too. I really hope she did get rid of all the moon water though . . . for Claire's sake at least. And I guess Luna was never really like Sylvia anyway. Luna didn't want to hurt people."

"Not wanting to doesn't mean she didn't," I say. "So what's the story? What are we going to tell everyone we did at camp this summer? Once again, the reality is too wild to believe."

"Well . . . you got your first sort-of kiss," Nora says, her voice on the verge of squealing.

My neck and chest feel like they're on fire. I told Nora that night after all the campers had transformed back and she shrieked so loudly that a whole family of bats flew out of the tree above us. "Does the cheek even count?"

"Oh, it totally counts." She nods authoritatively. "And we almost had a dance, so I'm going to go ahead and check that off my list too. Oh! Our friendship bracelets survived the last two weeks, which is sort of amazing."

I look down at my bracelet. It really is amazing.

CHAPTER TWENTY-EIGHT
Nora

As I wind down the now-familiar path toward the abandoned boathouse on the final day of camp, I'm a whole storm of emotions.

I'm relieved that Camp Sylvania's supernatural madness has come to an end, excited to get back to my real life and sleep in my own bed again, and sad that I'll have to say goodbye to everyone who has become such a fixture in my day-to-day these last two weeks.

Even though I may not have gotten my first kiss or a so-called normal summer camp experience (whatever that is!), I'm grateful for the things I did get: new friends, more confidence, a renewed connection with Maggie, and a summer I won't forget (EVER).

When I arrive at the boathouse, Claire is stretched out in one of the old canoes outside, her legs dangling over the side as she reads a book called *Howl Ya Doin'? The Ultimate Guide to Werewolves*. It reminds me so much of that first time I saw her looking super cool and confident, though I know now she was dealing with her own things—the same as any of us.

"Now *that's* an interesting choice for a book," I tease.

Claire looks up and offers a sheepish grin. "I thought it might be good to learn more about werewolves given—well, everything. Plus, Mom's been talking about hanging on to the camp rather than selling. She might turn it into some kind of nature preserve for paranormal kids."

"Seriously?"

"Who knows with her?" Claire shrugs, closing the book. "But I'm glad you came."

"I wouldn't leave without saying goodbye." I slip into the seat across from her. "Not after everything we've been through!"

"Are you saying you don't spend every summer dealing with werewolves? Amateur," she jokes. "And I'm still sorry, you know."

I nod. "Yeah, I know. Would it make you feel better if I said we could start over?"

Her face brightens. "Really?"

"Really." I hold out a hand to hers. "Hi, I'm Nora. I like fashion and theater and have a secret collection of stuffed animals."

Claire laughs as she shakes my hand. "Claire. I'm into coding and books—especially manga—and music. Oh! And my favorite color is black."

I pretend to be shocked. "You don't say!" Then I smile.

"Let's keep in touch, okay?"

"Definitely. You have my email. And maybe you can mail me one of your infamous handwritten letters!"

"Defally," I say, a reference back to the beginning of camp. We both laugh.

There's rustling from behind us and a voice shouts, "INCOMING!"

A rush of cool water suddenly splashes down my back and I gasp. When I glance over at Claire, her whole head is drenched, black and blue hair hanging in limp strands.

"Oh, it is so on!" Claire shouts. She scrambles to her feet and chases after the Big Liams, who run away cackling and holding colorful, water-filled balloons. Elijah, who's holding a couple of his own water balloons, waves at me.

I wave back, walking toward him. "Hard to believe we have to go back to normal after all this, huh?"

"Yeah. I still get serious cravings for raw meat, and I don't think that's gonna fly with my moms," Elijah says with a laugh. He pieced together the werewolf thing on his own since he already knew about Maggie's theory, so Claire filled in the blanks for him. "Kind of a bummer we never got to go to the Moon Ball."

"Totally. But maybe we can keep in touch?"

Elijah smiles at me. "That would be cool."

I reach into my pocket and pull out a mini notebook and pen. "Write down your email for me?"

He hands me his water balloons so he can. But as Elijah

goes to hand me back the items, I hold on to one of the water balloons I'd been holding for him. (Just filled with regular water and not moon water to be clear.)

"Your friends threw one of these at me and Claire, so it only seems fair that I pay you back," I say with a grin. "How fast can you run?"

"You wouldn't," Elijah challenges.

I wind my arm back, ready for aim. "Oh, but I would!"

Elijah takes off laughing and I laugh, too, throwing as hard as I can. Water explodes on his shoulder as the balloon pops.

Apparently, some parts of camp never change.

I sure did though.

After I've said my goodbyes to Logan and Jesse, to Birdie, to Claire and Luna, and to the Big Liams and Elijah, all that's left to do is wait for Mami and Stepdad Steve to pick me up. Maggie's parents are picking her up, and I'll see her back home in just a few days. I hear my mom before I see her.

"There's my baby!" Mami squeals.

"Mami!" I run to her, forgetting any sense of "cool" I tried to convey when I first arrived. I throw my arms around her in a huge hug, taking a deep breath. Her familiar smell of coconut shampoo and cocoa butter lotion fills my nose. Home. "I missed you."

"You have *no idea*, mija." She squeezes me so hard I feel like I might break in half, but I don't mind. "The house has been so quiet without you belting out show tunes."

"Don't you worry," I promise. "We have the whole ride home for that."

"That's what I was hoping you would say!" Mami smooths my hair and kisses my forehead before moving to grab my luggage.

"Can't we make Stepdad Steve do that?" I ask.

"I mean, we could, but we'd be waiting an awfully long time. I left Steve at home. Darren too. Thought we might enjoy a nice girl's trip home. I missed having just me-and-you time." She puts her hands on her hips. "What do you say?"

"YES!" I clap my hands together excitedly. "Ooh, can we take the long way home?"

Mami starts loading my bags into the back seat of our car. "Why not?"

I toss a duffel next to my suitcase. "And can we do some shopping along the way?"

"That was a given," Mami says, as we climb into the front seat.

"And can I *finally* get a cell phone?"

She shoots me a look. "Now you're pushing it."

"Oh, fine." I buckle my seat belt and let out a dramatic sigh so she knows I'm only playing. "But just so you know, I'm going to spend the whole trip home trying to convince you to change your mind."

Mami laughs, shaking her head. "I would expect nothing less."

She eases the car down the dirt road and I take in all the sights I'd come to know: the lavender garland, the now-empty area where the moon-water pool lived, the cabins labeled with phases of the moon, the barn where the contraband had been stored. I even spot Maggie walking down to the abandoned boathouse, and it makes me smile to myself. We really had a wild couple of weeks, some days that tested us more than others, but we came out on the other side better and stronger.

To my surprise, I realize that some part of me is going to miss this place—but knowing Mami missed me just as much as I missed her makes me think this upcoming school year, and our new life with Stepdad Steve and Darren, might not be so bad.

Whatever happens, I know myself better now, and I've got my best friend. As far as I'm concerned, that's all I need.

CHAPTER TWENTY-NINE
Maggie

Kit and Evelyn left first thing this morning for the airport, so it was just me packing up the rest of my stuff by myself as I wait for Mom and Dad.

I'm scanning the cabin for any last things I might leave behind when my door rattles with a knock. "Come in," I call.

Birdie steps inside, holding a very familiar plastic baggie up for me to see. "I come bearing toiletries," she says.

"Thanks!" I catch them as she tosses the bag. "I sort of forgot about these after I got my EMF reader."

Birdie nods. "Yeah, toiletries are way more boring than that."

I haven't really had a chance to talk to Birdie much since I transformed back. "Thanks for, um, howling at me the other day at your cabin. I felt so scared and alone . . . but it was nice to know I had a pack."

Birdie sits down on the edge of Evelyn's now stripped bed. "It was the least I could do. I bought into Luna's moon-water dreams without thinking twice, and I could have stopped all of this, but—"

"It's okay," I say.

Birdie blushes. "I just really wanted to believe in something. The moon water seemed harmless and for a while, it made me feel good. And Luna . . . well, I thought she was pretty cool too."

"Oh, Birdie," I plop down next to her. "I guess the good news is that Luna isn't all bad."

"People hardly ever are," she says dreamily, and I'm pretty sure it's safe to say that Birdie's crush hasn't been cured. "Maybe we can do the camp thing again some time."

"Maybe," I tell her. "I might need a break from the wilderness."

"Who knows?" Birdie shrugs. "Maybe next summer we can get abducted by aliens?"

"Okay, but only if I'm back in time for the first day of school."

"That's a guarantee, Maggie Bananas."

"Hey there," I say as I approach Logan sitting in the grass near the boathouse. "Looks like this place is just about cleared out."

Logan pats the ground and I sit beside him. Goose bumps trail up my arms as my nerves start to take over. This is the first time we've been truly alone since the barn a few days ago. What if all that happened that day was just a onetime thing and it's faded now?

"I know I shouldn't, between the vampire takeovers and werewolf infestations, but I'm really going to miss this place," he says.

I look out at the perfectly still lake, the reflection of the clouds rippling over the top. "Yeah, I think it's safe to say that Camp Sylvania has sunk its fangs into us."

He grins. "And its claws."

In an attempt to play it super cool, I pretend to ignore his hand slowly inching toward mine until our pinkies just barely touch. I gulp silently as my stomach does backflips. Is this what growing up is like? I don't think I'm cut out for it.

But also, I can't wait to tell Nora.

Logan clears his throat and pulls his hand back. "I, uh, made you something." He proceeds to dig into his pocket before pulling out a multicolored origami bracelet, which he then slides over my wrist. "It's made out of candy wrappers from the contraband we used to spoil the moon water."

The bracelet sits right next to Nora's and my friendship bracelet and they are by far the two coolest things I own. Not including my EMF reader, which basically saved the day. "This is so sweet," I say, my lips spreading into a goofy smile. "Like in a cool way. But also, in a sweet way."

"Yeah?" he asks. "You really like it?"

"I love it," I assure him.

He bites down on his lip. "So, I'm getting a phone when I go home. Maybe I could email you my number and we could talk."

"I would really like that," I tell him. "I might get a phone for my birthday this year, so we could text then too."

"Prepare yourself to be flooded with memes," he promises.

"I'm so ready."

We sit there in silence for a while longer, and this time he reaches out and holds my hand without any hesitation.

Play it cool, I beg myself.

All around us, the campwide intercom system crackles to life as radio stations flip back and forth before finally landing on a super-old-sounding song like it could be straight out of *Grease.*

The croony voice sings, *"And they call it puppy love . . ."*

"Seriously, Howie?" I shout.

Logan chuckles but doesn't let go of my hand. "Let the guy have his fun."

After the song finishes, I hear tires on the gravel road at the top of the hill and immediately recognize my parents' car.

It's time to say goodbye to this place.

At the start of all this, the only thing I cared about was discovering supernatural secrets, and Nora just wanted a totally normal summer camp experience. But in the end, Nora learned to harness the paranormal and I walked away with my first kiss. Neither of us ever saw that coming.

But that's the thing about Camp Sylvania: it's always full of surprises.

ACKNOWLEDGMENTS
Julie

Going back to camp has been a dream!

Thank you so much to Crystal for jumping on board to tell Nora's story. It's been such a treat to collaborate with a writer I admire so much!

I am so lucky to work on yet another project with my editor, Alessandra Balzer, the fiercest in the biz.

John and Mary, what can I say? Bittersweet was just a dream, and you two have made it a reality. I can't wait to see what stories the future holds for us.

Thank you to my Harper family for being the best team a gal could ask for.

To my family and friends who don't mind when I disappear for chunks at a time to write but who are always there when I resurface, I am so, so grateful for each of you.

Lastly, to Ian, my love, I think it's time we take the cats on a camping trip. They would hate it. Love you.

Crystal

Like Nora needs Maggie, every good book needs a good team. I am so grateful to the team who helped make this book happen.

Thank you to our editor, Alessandra Balzer, for seeing the value in this story and for offering your insightful notes and wonderful guidance.

Thank you to the entire team at HarperCollins and Balzer + Bray for championing this story.

To the Bittersweet Books team, including John Cusick and Mary Kole, I can't thank you enough for welcoming me to Camp Sylvania.

To my brilliant agent-slash-occasional-therapist, Tamar Rydzinski, who is always willing to talk me through just about anything, thank you for always reminding me to go after what I want.

Thank you to the loveliest Monica Rodriguez for generously humoring me with marketing and social ideas and for sending me the best TikToks.

If you fell in love with the cover of this book, SAME, and a huge thank-you to the talented Emma Cormarie, who did the jacket art; Alix Northrup, who did the lettering; and Jenna Stempel-Lobell, who did the jacket design.

To readers, librarians, booksellers, students, teachers, professors, the bookish community on social media, book clubs, and book lovers everywhere, thank you for all you do.

To Julie Murphy, who gave me the surprise of a lifetime by inviting me to co-write a book, thank you. *Dumplin'* is one of the books that inspired me to become an author, so writing this book together felt like the ultimate somebody-pinch-me moment. I now love Maggie, Nora, and the whole Camp Sylvania family like they're my own. Thanks for sharing them with me. I've always wanted to go to camp, and now I can say I've been!

To Olivia Abtahi, Angela Velez, Kate Albus, Kerri Vautour, Cait Roberts, Judy Kelliher, Jane Johnson Vottero, Kristen Brosius, Angela Veatch, Paige Moran, Laraine Robison, Deleney Magoffin, Liz Reddinger, Sanya Sagar, Kimberly Ashcraft, and all of my incredible friends: thanks for sticking with me through all the beautiful and chaotic phases of life.

Thank you to all of my family, with a special shout-out to my brother, Lorenzo, and my father-in-law, Bill, for always taking the time to celebrate me and my books.

To Obi, for snuggling in my lap whenever I'm on deadline.

To Maya, who reminds me every day of the importance of dreaming big and making time for laughing and snuggling.

And to Bubby, the love of my life and my first (and biggest) supporter: this is only possible because of you. Fighting werewolves doesn't sound too scary as long as I have you by my side.